THE
BREAKFAST CLUB ADVENTURES

THE HEADLESS GHOST

This book belongs to

Books by Marcus Rashford

Fiction

written with Alex Falase-Koya

The Breakfast Club Adventures: The Beast Beyond the Fence
The Breakfast Club Adventures: The Ghoul in the School
The Breakfast Club Adventures: The Phantom Thief
The Breakfast Club Adventures: The Treasure Hunt Monster

Non-Fiction

written with Carl Anka

You Are a Champion: How to Be the Best You Can Be
You Can Do It: How to Find Your Voice and
Make a Difference
Heroes: How to Turn Inspiration into Action

written with Katie Warriner

You Are a Champion Action Planner: 50 Activities to
Achieve Your Dreams

MACMILLAN CHILDREN'S BOOKS

MARCUS RASHFORD

Written with Isaac Hamilton-McKenzie • Illustrated by Marta Kissi

THE BREAKFAST CLUB ADVENTURES

THE HEADLESS GHOST

Published 2024 by Macmillan Children's Books
an imprint of Pan Macmillan
The Smithson, 6 Briset Street, London EC1M 5NR
EU representative: Macmillan Publishers Ireland Ltd, 1st Floor,
The Liffey Trust Centre, 117–126 Sheriff Street Upper
Dublin 1, D01 YC43
Associated companies throughout the world
www.panmacmillan.com

ISBN 978-1-0350-5394-0

Text copyright © MUCS Enterprises Limited 2024
Illustrations copyright © Marta Kissi 2024

The right of Marcus Rashford and Marta Kissi to be identified as the
author and illustrator of this work has been asserted by them
in accordance with the Copyright, Designs and Patents Act 1988.

1 3 5 7 9 8 6 4 2

A CIP catalogue record for this book is available from the British Library.

Printed and bound by CPI Group (UK) Ltd, Croydon CR0 4YY

To every child who attends Breakfast Club,

this is your starting point.

The world is full of possibilities,

you just have to let your mind take you there.

Chapter One

Marcus sprinted out of the penalty area, tracking the ball overhead as it floated towards Tomas's right foot.

'Block it, Marcus!' yelled his friend and teammate, Oyin, from his left.

Marcus closed in, but he was too late. Tomas volleyed the ball with a **THUMP,** sending it flying towards the goal. Patrick, their goalkeeper, didn't stand a chance.

As the net bulged, Marcus's shoulders slumped. Watching the team of boys and girls from Year Nine celebrate their equalizer was a **GUT-PUNCH**. The goal set their grudge match at two goals apiece, and there were only a few minutes of lunchtime break left.

'Stay focused, guys!' urged Oyin. She hurried to the centre circle, eager to kick off again.

'We can still win this!' yelled Patrick, nudging his glasses back in place.

Marcus wasn't so sure. He'd never say it out loud, but their rivals were *good*. Older and more experienced, the team of Year Nines had the upper hand and Marcus's team of Year Eight players hadn't won a single match against them all week!

As Oyin set the ball on the centre spot,

Marcus glanced at the large group gathering on the sidelines. Their game had the entire school watching. He quickly searched the crowd for his friends and fellow **Breakfast Club Investigators**, Lise, Asim and Stacey, but they weren't there.

'So not the entire school,' Marcus murmured to himself.

He was disappointed but not surprised. Ever since the creation of Drama Club last month, the **BCI** had barely met up.

Drama Club was the newest and most popular club at Rutherford School. For a split second, Marcus had thought about signing up, but he had never really liked drama, or the spotlight. He preferred the action of the pitch far more.

Anyway, Drama Club had filled up almost

immediately. Many students had left other clubs to join the stage. Marcus's Investigator friends became so busy with Drama Club that the **BCI** hadn't solved any mysteries or taken on a new case in ages.

Marcus felt his chest tighten. The **BCI** was the main thing that brought him, Lise, Stacey and Asim together, and with Drama Club keeping them busy, the four of them hadn't had time for their usual meet-ups.

'Marcus!'

Patrick's shout **JOLTED** Marcus from his thoughts. Patrick had lobbed the ball towards him, sending it hurtling in the direction of his head.

Marcus sprang back, just in time before the football smacked him in the face. He took the ball on his chest, then clamped it under his foot. He realized this was not the time to be thinking about the **BCI** or Drama Club. He had to focus on the match.

He set the ball out ahead of him, dribbling down the left wing. He glided to the right, narrowly avoiding a crunching tackle. The crowd roared and **CHEERED** in the background as Marcus kept on, weaving his way past a second and then a third defender. He chopped the ball with the outside of his foot, and the crowd gasped and cheered even louder.

'The lunch bell is about to go!' shouted a voice from the crowd.

'He's never gonna make it!' yelled another.

Marcus knew he only had seconds left, and there was one last defender to beat: Tomas.

Tomas gave him a smug smile, showing

white, even teeth. Marcus wasn't worried. Tomas was weak with his left foot, and Marcus knew how to exploit that. He knocked the ball to the left, just far enough to make Tomas reach, before cutting back to his right. Tomas fell, and Marcus took his shot, driving a long-range effort straight at the top corner.

The net rippled.

Then the crowd erupted.

'GOAALLLLL!'

Marcus's team rushed around him, celebrating in a chaotic circle, just as the bell began to ring.

'Top bins!' cried out Oyin.

'What a banger, Marcus!' congratulated Patrick.

Marcus smiled so wide, his cheeks ached, as Tomas and the Year Nines trudged off the pitch. Winning felt SWEET.

Chapter Two

Marcus walked into school, his football tucked firmly under his arm. He had probably never scored a better goal during a lunchtime match, so why didn't he feel happier?

'What a game,' Patrick said, running to catch up with Marcus. Oyin was by his side.

'You can say that again,' chipped in Oyin. 'Did you see their faces? I've been waiting all week to beat the Year Nines.'

Marcus nodded. 'I'm just happy we won.'

Oyin nudged him.

Marcus smiled. 'OK, I'm *really* happy we won.' Even though he missed spending time with the **Breakfast Club Investigators**, it was good to know he still had Patrick and Oyin. After discovering that Oyin and Patrick had been responsible for the **Spoiler** – a giant alien who had terrorized Rutherford School a few weeks ago – Marcus was worried their friendship was ruined. But after talking it through, the three of them were as close as ever.

Patrick put a hand on Marcus's shoulder as they walked through the double doors and towards class. 'Wanna go to the Cage tomorrow?' he asked. 'We should practise for next week. Tomas's team will want revenge.'

'Sounds good,' Marcus said, smiling.

Oyin and Patrick turned left and headed towards the Maths classrooms together, but Marcus had English after lunch so went right. As he walked down the corridor, he heard **laughter** spilling into the hallway from one of the rooms. It was coming from the old school theatre where Drama Club met during lunch and after school. The laughing got louder as Marcus neared the open door, and just as he got close enough to peer inside, Stacey, Asim and Lise BURST OUT. They were giggling, looking down at a folder Stacey was holding open and not watching where they were going.

OOF!

Stacey bumped right into Marcus, knocking the football out from under his arm. She dropped her folder and bits of paper flew everywhere, scattering on the floor.

'*Marcus!*' Stacey cried. She sounded annoyed.

'Wait a sec,' Marcus said. 'You walked into me!'

Stacey made a humph sound and bent down to pick up her folder.

'What is this?' Marcus asked, picking up some of the sheets strewn around them.

'They're scripts for the play Drama Club is putting on,' Stacey said excitedly. She coughed and looked encouragingly at Lise.

Lise was grinning proudly. 'THE GHOST OF RUTHERFORD SCHOOL,' she said in a spooky voice. 'Written by yours truly.'

Marcus's brows raised. 'You wrote this, for real?' he asked, amazed.

Lise shrugged humbly. 'It's inspired by my experiences in the BCI. It's about a ghost, and a fearless ghost hunter who tracks it down.'

'Wow, that sounds brilliant,' Marcus said, impressed.

'And I'm in charge of set design,' Asim chimed in. 'I'll get to craft all the scenery. Paint the background, design the fake school. It's going to be a masterpiece!'

Stacey grabbed Marcus's arm excitedly. 'And guess what I'm doing?' she said.

Marcus felt overwhelmed by their enthusiasm. Stacey was holding onto his arm really tightly. 'Um . . .' he began.

'—I'm the director!' Stacey blared, so excited she could barely stand still.

Marcus looked at the three of them grinning from ear to ear. He was proud of them, but also felt a bit left out that they were doing something so exciting without him.

'Guys, that's really great. I ho—' He broke off as he heard the familiar sharp clacking of heels. Their headteacher, Mrs Miller, was approaching. She loomed over them as she came to a stop. Usually, Mrs Miller wore a suspicious look on her angular face when it came to the BCI, but once her eyes locked onto Lise's script, she actually looked pleased.

'I've heard a lot of good things about this script,' Mrs Miller said. 'And I'm delighted that Drama Club's first production will be written by a student.'

Lise's cheeks went a bit red, but Marcus could tell she was flattered.

'Thank you, Mrs Miller,' Lise said.

Mrs Miller nodded curtly. 'Of course, there's a lot resting on it too,' she added.

'There is?' asked Asim. His voice came out as a squeak.

Mrs Miller raised an eyebrow. 'Well, it's the first time we're charging for tickets, and the money raised will be donated to Rutherford's ***Journey Youth Theatre*** for young people that might not have access to drama classes. A lot of great creatives have passed through their programmes, and we wouldn't want to let them down.'

Stacey stood to attention. 'We won't, Mrs Miller. I promise. This play is going to sell out.'

'We'll see,' Mrs Miller said with a nod before marching down the hall. None of the Investigators said a word until she turned the corner.

Asim let out a breath. 'Even when Mrs Miller is congratulating us, she still makes me nervous.'

Marcus laughed. It was true. You definitely needed to be on the ball when the headteacher was around!

'My football!' Marcus gasped, suddenly remembering that it had gone flying when he'd bumped into Stacey. 'Did you see where it went?' he asked, but all three of his friends gave him a blank look.

Marcus sighed in *FRUSTRATION* and scanned the corridor.

He spotted two students strolling out from the theatre. A tall boy with fair skin, red hair and freckles, and a girl with long black braids and brown skin.

Marcus felt his shoulders drop in relief as they got closer because the girl was holding Marus's football. He opened his mouth, eager to get it back, but the girl was already talking.

'Hey, Stacey, did I hear you guys talking

to Mrs Miller?' she asked.

Stacey nodded. 'Turns out there's a lot more riding on this performance than we thought, Adeya. It's got to be perfect. And we need to sell as many tickets as we can to raise money for charity.'

Adeya seemed like she wanted to say

something, but she stayed silent. Then she turned to Marcus, and **THREW** him his football. 'Hey, I'm Adeya. Were you looking for this?'

'Yes, thanks,' Marcus replied. He'd seen Adeya play football before, she had really good technique. Her dribbling ability was one of the best at Rutherford, and she was a great athlete too. When she ran, her feet barely touched the ground. It was like she was floating. 'I've seen you on the pitch, right?' he asked.

'Yeah,' said Adeya, turning to her friend. 'And this is Lawson. He plays football too when he can be dragged from the stage.'

Lawson waved. 'I can't help it if I'm born to perform!'

'You should have played this lunch break,' Marcus said. 'It was a really good game.'

'For real?' Adeya said. 'I—'

'Adeya doesn't have time for football,' Stacey interrupted. 'She's the *star of the show*, the ghost hunter in our play!'

'Good point,' Asim said seriously. 'You'll need to focus, Adeya. There are a lot of lines to learn.'

Everyone turned to Adeya, waiting for her to say something, but no words came.

'The ghost hunter, Adeya?' Marcus said quickly, filling the silence. 'Nice one!'

'Thanks,' Adeya replied. 'It's my first time acting in anything. I only signed up to Drama Club because Lawson wanted me to. I never expected to land the lead role.'

'That just shows how good you are,' said Lise. 'A natural talent.'

'I guess.' Adeya shrugged.

'And you're going to be great,' Lawson said, putting his arm around Adeya. 'You're so lucky to have the main part. Although my role is pretty cool – I'm playing the ghost!' He wiggled his fingers **spookily** and everyone laughed, except Adeya.

'You're right, I'm really lucky . . . How many lines is it, Lise?' Adeya asked.

But before Lise could answer, Stacey butted in again.

'You've got the most lines in the whole show! I'll run through them with you until you've learned them perfectly.' Stacey took Adeya by the arm and swept her down the hallway. 'I'll walk with you to class and we can start practising now.'

Adeya shot an unsure look over at Lawson and mouthed the word 'Bye' apologetically.

Lawson shook his head with a smile and hurried off in the opposite direction.

'I guess we should go too, we don't want to be late for English,' Lise said to Marcus and Asim.

As they walked, Marcus wanted to tell them about his epic lunchtime goal, but they were too busy discussing the play.

Chapter Three

The last class of the day went by in a flash and Marcus still felt a bit low as he headed for the school exit. He'd really wanted to share the story of the lunchtime match with his friends, but they were so distracted by the play he hadn't had a chance.

Marcus felt a yank on his arm. 'Hey! Hold up, Marcus!' It was Lise. 'Didn't you hear me calling you?'

'Sorry,' Marcus said distractedly. 'I was thinking about some stuff.'

'No problem. Do you fancy coming to watch our rehearsals?' Lise asked.

Surprised by her offer, but excited to see what his friends had been up to, Marcus agreed.

Lise smiled. 'Great! We all really want you to see what we've been working on. Even if you're not part of Drama Club, we're still a **team,** remember?' She nudged his arm, and Marcus couldn't help but smile. Lise making the effort to include him definitely made him feel better.

Walking into the theatre, Marcus noticed the room **BUZZED** with activity. People ran around with costumes, cables for the spotlights and furniture for the stage. It was like getting a proper peek behind the scenes.

Asim was painting the set. He was so quiet it was like he was **HYPNOTIZED** by his brush as he dipped it into a paint can.

Marcus and Lise stood behind Stacey, who sat cross-legged on a director's chair in front of the stage. She was clearly embracing her role and wore a purple beret which definitely made her look the part.

'Hey, Marcus,' said Stacey, looking over her shoulder while still *twirling* a pen between her fingers. 'I see you've come to watch our masterpiece.'

Marcus smiled, but before he could even respond, Stacey whipped around in her chair. 'Clear the stage!' she called out. 'Adeya, let's give that last scene another try.'

Asim left his paint can behind the old curtain and then came to join them behind Stacey's seat. Marcus's gaze panned across the room to a flustered-looking Adeya, who wore a long cloak that looked like it might belong to Sherlock Holmes.

'Coming!' Adeya said. Her eyes were wide as she scurried up the stage steps, but she was in such a hurry she tripped on the stairs and fell to her knees.

Marcus winced. He felt sorry for her.

'S-s-sorry!' Adeya stuttered, scrambling to her feet. She wrapped her cloak back around her and found her position.

'How's Adeya been doing in rehearsals?' Marcus whispered to Lise.

'You'll see,' Lise answered.

Lise handed Stacey a clipboard, and Stacey

began reading out lines from the script theatrically. Marcus smiled at how much emphasis Stacey put on each sentence; she was taking her role of director very seriously.

'What's she doing?' he whispered to Asim.

'She's reading the lines that come before Adeya's. When she says, "Who can solve this mystery?" Adeya starts her big speech.'

Marcus nodded and listened as Stacey made her way through the script.

'Who can solve this mystery?' Stacey said dramatically. There was a pause and Stacey tried again. 'I said, "Who can solve this mystery?" . . . Adeya, that's your cue!'

'Oh, sorry!' Adeya said, with an embarrassed smile. 'I didn't realize.'

'No worries . . .' Stacey said patiently. 'Just take your time, all right? And remember, you're a **BRAVE** ghost hunter! Say everything confidently!'

Adeya took in a deep breath and gave a thumbs up. Stacey started over, but this time read the lines a little slower.

However, each time it was Adeya's cue to speak, she still couldn't remember a thing. Whenever Stacey said her line, it took Adeya a few seconds to even realize it was her turn.

'Can you remind me what I'm supposed to say?' Adeya asked in a small voice after the fifth run-through.

Stacey smiled, but it looked strained. 'Why don't you have a break? We'll try another scene while you try to memorize your lines.'

Adeya nodded meekly. 'Oh . . . OK,' she said.

Marcus felt bad for Adeya as she walked off the stage, her head hung low. Stacey hadn't been unkind, but performing on the stage looked really tough. It was no wonder Adeya seemed so anxious. Marcus knew he could never remember all those lines.

Stacey clicked her fingers impatiently and called up the next group of actors. Lawson got into character, draping a sheet over his head as he climbed the steps. The other actors were playing students, wearing their school uniforms and schoolbags.

'We're performing scene five!' Stacey bellowed. 'Our horrifying GHOST has appeared in the school for the first time. Lawson, heavy on the scary! And the rest of you, I want to *believe* you are frightened for your lives. Three . . . two . . . one . . . **ACT!'**

At once, the actors came to life. Lawson prowled forwards, waving his arms and making ghoulish **woooo**! noises as he chased the other actors relentlessly around the stage.

Marcus knew it was supposed to be scary, but he couldn't help but laugh. It was like watching a funny cartoon, not a scary horror film. Lawson waved his arms like he was

disco dancing, and the noises he made weren't exactly chilling.

Suddenly, the lights in the theatre began to flicker, plunging the room into darkness for seconds at a time. A spooky clanging noise, like the clanking of chains, invaded the theatre, echoing and bouncing off the walls.

Marcus stopped laughing. This was more like it!

Now the actors being chased looked truly petrified, and even though Marcus knew the effects were for the play, he felt his heart begin to race.

Marcus's heart beat even faster when he saw Lawson remove his ghost costume. His green eyes flashed with FEAR and he looked genuinely terrified.

In fact, the entire room erupted into pure chaos.

Marcus turned to look at Lise and Stacey. 'This isn't part of the play, is it?' he said slowly.

His friends shook their heads in unison.

'Run for your lives!' Lawson shrieked as he pushed past the actors and fled down the stage steps. He darted past them towards the exit. 'The theatre is **haunted!'**

Chapter Four

'Everybody calm down!' urged Stacey. The beret fell from her head as she leaped from her chair and marched up the stage steps. Through the flickering lights, Marcus watched her disappear behind the stage's left wing.

'Where's she going?' Marcus asked Asim and Lise. He could barely hear himself over the clanking of chains and **shrieks** of students that filled the theatre.

All at once, the lights stopped flashing and the rattling noises came to a halt. Stacey strode from behind the curtain with her hands on her hips. 'Everyone gather around!' she demanded.

Marcus looked around him as actors popped out from their hiding spots. Even Lawson peeled himself from behind the theatre door and shuffled to the foot of the stage.

Asim threw Stacey's purple beret up to her and she pulled it onto her head forcefully.

'Look, guys, we know this theatre is old and rarely used. The curtains have moths, the stage is RICKETY and the lights playing up is just a fault in the circuits. Or someone probably kicked a switch by accident.'

'B-b-but what about the noises?' stuttered Lawson.

The other actors nodded nervously behind him.

Stacey shrugged. 'It was probably just the wind from the open windows or old pipes. Noise travels easily in here, we all know that.'

Lawson bit his bottom lip but nodded.

Marcus, however, was stunned. He couldn't believe what he was hearing. Stacey, a girl whose favourite book was *An Encyclopaedia of the Supernatural*, was trying to downplay the possibility of something being **spooky?** Stacey was always the one trying to convince them that anything strange had a paranormal explanation!

'OK, back in your positions everyone!'

Stacey announced. 'Let's get scene five pitch-perfect before the end of today's rehearsal.'

While Stacey urged the actors back on stage, Marcus turned to Lise and Asim.

'So what do you think? Is the theatre haunted?' Marcus asked.

'I hope not,' Lise replied mournfully. 'If that's true, then there's a chance the play won't be shown. I worked too hard on that script for a GHOST to mess it all up.'

'And I've already spent hours painting the set!' Asim added grimly. 'That'd all be for nothing if the show got cancelled . . . I reckon Stacey's right, it's probably the pipes.'

Lise nodded in agreement, but Marcus wasn't ready to let it go. 'But shouldn't we investigate it . . . you know, just to be sure?' he asked. 'This seems like a perfect case for the **Breakfast Club Investigators**.'

Lise and Asim locked eyes, leaving the three of them in an awkward silence. Marcus could tell they weren't keen to investigate, or perhaps they were more interested in the play. Either way, the **BCI** didn't seem like they would be making a comeback any time soon. He felt a surge of disappointment.

Marcus cleared his throat. 'Anyway, how are the ticket sales for the play going?' he asked, changing the subject. 'Didn't Mrs Miller say any money raised would go to the Youth Theatre project?'

Marcus thought he saw a flash of worry in Lise's eyes. 'Not the best so far, but I'm sure they'll pick up soon,' she said hopefully.

'Well, we'd better get back to it!' Stacey said with a smile.

Marcus stood alone, watching his friends walk back towards the stage. He knew a case when he saw one, and there was undoubtedly something going on with those flickering lights and clanking noises. The only way he could find out for certain was by staying close to Drama Club and the theatre. Even if he had to do it alone, he would get to the bottom of what was going on.

Chapter Five

Stacey snapped her fingers impatiently. 'Don't worry about the distractions, people. As they say in the entertainment business, "The show must go on!"'

Lawson shrugged his shoulders. 'Haven't we done enough rehearsals today, Stacey? It's getting late, and I'm starving.'

The other actors let out a hungry groan at the mention of eating. To be fair, it was more than an hour and a half after the end of the school day, and even though Marcus was just watching the rehearsal, he was beginning to feel tired and hungry too.

'*What?* No, we are just hitting our stride!' Stacey exclaimed. 'Push through, guys, we've almost nailed the scene—'

'Maybe they have a point, Stacey,' Lise interrupted. 'No one can rehearse at their best when they're tired or on an empty stomach. I suggest we come back next week, fresh and ready to go again.'

'I don't know,' Stacey said, running an anxious eye over her clipboard.

'Actually, I really do have to go!' declared Adeya, standing up in the corner, looking anxiously at her phone.

Only then did Marcus realize he hadn't

seen Adeya in a while. She must have been studying her lines.

'I'm supposed to be helping my mum with the shopping tonight.'

Outnumbered, Stacey took off her beret. 'Fine. Rehearsals are done for the day. All of you get some rest and we'll start again on Monday.'

A collective exhale bounced off the walls. Asim and Lise joined the rest of Drama Club, putting away the set and props and returning their costumes to the clothes racks.

Stacey went to chase after Adeya, with her clipboard, highlighter and more suggestions for her performance, but Adeya was faster and managed to slip out of the theatre's doors.

Marcus was waiting by the doors for Asim to pack up so they could walk home together when he overheard an interesting conversation from two of the actors playing scared students.

'I don't care what Stacey thinks, those noises weren't normal,' whispered a short boy Marcus recognized from Maths. His voice **WOBBLED** as he spoke.

'I thought so too,' agreed his friend, 'There's no way I'm going backstage. I've heard rumours of . . .'

But Marcus didn't hear the rest as the two of them hurried to leave. He was pleased he wasn't the only one that could tell something **strange** was going on. Why couldn't the rest of the **BCI** see it?

'Is everyone packed up and ready?' Stacey called out from the wing of the stage. Seeing all the tired nods, she switched off the main overhead lights. A dusky, dim shade of orange took over the hall and suddenly it all felt a lot **spookier**. A faint clanking noise echoed through the theatre.

'What's that?' Marcus said.

Asim and Lise *narrowed* their eyes and Stacey stopped in the middle of the stage. 'What's what?' asked Stacey.

The peculiar clanking grew louder until it was unmistakable. A *HAUNTING* howl of **WOOOHOOO** followed quickly behind it, shaking Marcus to his core.

'The ghost is underneath the stage!' cried one of the actors, and for the second time panic erupted. The remaining kids screamed as they bolted for the exit, leaving just Marcus, Lise and Asim with Stacey in the theatre.

This time even Stacey looked **spooked** and she didn't seem able to move from the stage.

Marcus, Lise and Asim rushed up the steps and formed a circle with Stacey, their backs to each other. The clanging noise got so loud it made the stage **vibrate** and suddenly a harsh creak screeched from beneath the floor.

'What's happening?' shouted Marcus. He took in a tight, shallow breath.

The clanging continued and Asim let loose a *SQUEAL*. He pointed to a section of the stage where wisps of smoke rose from the wooden floor.

A trapdoor lifted

slowly, releasing a cloudy fog that scudded over their heads.

Suddenly, the clanking stopped.

A silence took over, and somehow, the lack of noise was even worse. Marcus shivered and felt his friends trembling too. But nothing appeared from the trapdoor.

'Do you think it's gone?' Lise whispered.

'Maybe,' Marcus offered. 'But how do we know for sur—'

'BEEEE GONNNE!' roared a voice, deep and angry. It reverberated around them, swamping their ears like an overbearing wave. The fog in the air seemed to channel the creepiness, snaking and twisting around them.

'RUN!' Asim cried, his heavy footsteps filling the theatre as he fled.

Lise and Stacey hurried after him down the stairs, while Marcus leaped from the stage, through the doors and down the corridor. Their screams ECHOED off the walls, and it wasn't until they reached the school gates that any of them stopped for breath.

'That settles it,' Marcus declared, in between short, tired pants. 'I know this play means a lot to you all, but we *have* to investigate this.'

Chapter Six

The next day was Saturday, so Marcus, Oyin and Patrick met at the Cage near Marcus's block of flats. The Cage could be packed on the weekend, but today it was just the three of them. They were practising their football skills: one-on-ones, passing and long-range finishing while taking turns in goal.

'C'mon, Marcus, shoot like you did

yesterday!' urged Patrick, throwing the ball back at him.

Seeing Marcus's scowl, Oyin laughed. 'You want to keep your fingers, Patrick?' she warned. 'Be careful what you ask for.'

Marcus grinned, lining up his next shot at goal, when he heard the gate to the Cage click open. He glanced over his shoulder to see Adeya and Lawson walk onto the pitch.

'Get on with it!' Patrick called.

Focusing on the ball, Marcus flicked his eyes to the top corner of the goal and struck the ball with all his power. But the ball went flying over the bar, banging against the metal.

'What was that?' Oyin said, creasing over as she laughed. 'And after I bigged you up too!'

'I got distracted,' Marcus said, gesturing

towards Adeya and Lawson who were warming up on the other side of the Cage. 'I'll be back in a second,' he said, as he switched into Investigator mode and jogged towards the pair. Since the **BCI** had decided to look into the weird events in the school theatre, there was no harm in asking them a few questions about what had happened the day before.

'Hey!' Lawson said, as Marcus approached. He was sitting on the floor, stuffing his feet into his football boots.

Adeya was focused on her football as she **juggled** it on her knees. She waved at Marcus politely without looking away from the ball.

'How are you guys doing after yesterday?' Marcus asked. He tried his best not to sound too curious. He knew from previous cases that some people didn't take well to nosy questions. 'I was kind of spooked.'

'You can say that again.' Lawson *shivered*. 'I'm OK . . . I guess.'

Adeya didn't answer, she was busy counting her keepy-uppies under her breath.

'I know I'm new to Drama Club,' Marcus said, 'but things like that don't happen every week, do they?'

'Never,' Lawson scoffed. 'I've been in the club since it started, and nothing like this has ever happened.'

'That *is* strange. So why do you think it's happening now?' Marcus asked.

'*Well* . . .' Adeya said, letting the ball drop, 'my older brother once told me about a GHOST that haunted the theatre years ago.

The hauntings would get worse and worse as it got closer to opening night.' Her expression looked doubtful. 'I'd always thought they were silly stories, but now I'm wondering if there's some truth to them.'

'If the rumour is true, then what could've brought the GHOST back after all this time?' Marcus said, thoughtfully.

'Well, the theatre hadn't been used in ages until Drama Club started rehearsing a few weeks ago, so maybe we've disturbed it and it wants the theatre to itself,' Adeya suggested with a shrug.

Lawson jumped to his feet, one of his laces still untied. 'If that's true, then the ghost won't get its way,' he said. 'Stacey's not going to let **anything** stop the show.'

At Lawson's mention of Stacey, Marcus

frowned. 'What do you mean by that?' he asked.

'She just sent me a message, inviting me round to her house to go over my lines,' Adeya said, holding up her phone. 'She takes her job as director very seriously!'

'Oh, she told me she was too busy to hang out . . .' Marcus said.

'Stacey is never too busy when it comes to the play,' Lawson replied, bending down to tie his boot lace.

'Extra rehearsals sound like a good idea. If the GHOST doesn't ruin the play, Adeya, you'll need to learn those lines.'

Adeya let out a breath and nodded slowly. 'I know, I know. I guess I'll see you later.' She gently tapped the football to Lawson and began to walk away.

'Where are you going?' Marcus asked.

'To Stacey's house,' Adeya muttered. 'Lawson's right about my lines, football will have to wait.'

As Adeya SLUNK out of the Cage, Marcus thought about her brother's ghost story and bit his lip. If the ghost didn't want them to perform the play, and Stacey wouldn't give in, what would it do next to get what it wanted?

★

Sweaty and tired from football practice with Oyin and Patrick, Marcus walked home from the Cage. The longer he had played, the more **ANNOYED** he became that Stacey had put the play before the **BCI** this weekend.

When he had messaged the **BCI** group chat after school on Friday and asked if anyone was around at the weekend to talk about the case, Stacey had said she didn't have time. Marcus thought she might be busy with family, but now he knew she just wanted to rehearse with Adeya.

Marcus wondered if Lise and Asim were there too? They hadn't even replied to his message! He shook his head. Marcus knew he was being silly, but he missed having a crew who wanted to solve mysteries. The BCI was created for cases like this! Why was he the only one who remembered that?

Arriving home, Marcus took his trainers off and **DUMPED** himself on the living-room sofa. He heard his mum's footsteps coming down the hallway.

'Good game at the Cage?' she asked as she walked into the living room.

'Yeah, it was all right,' Marcus answered with a sigh.

'Just all right?' his mum asked, sitting down next to him.

'Yeah, I guess I couldn't really focus,' Marcus started and his mum looked at him, encouraging him to continue. 'Stacey, Lise and Asim are all working together on this new play for Drama Club.'

'Sounds fun,' said his mum. 'It's always good to try new things. So what's got you down?'

'It's not **FUN** for me, we barely hang out any more,' Marcus admitted. 'They're too busy with the play.'

'Ah, I see.' His mum gave him a sympathetic smile and shifted closer. 'You're feeling left out, is that it?'

Marcus gave a small nod and leaned on her shoulder.

'Do you remember when you had all that friendship trouble with Oyin and Patrick?' she said, gently lifting his chin. 'Friendship can take work, so have a think about what you could do to help your friends. And don't forget, when **challenges** come our way, true friends stand by each other.'

'But what if we're not as close as we used to be?' Marcus asked, his eyes wide with worry.

His mum kissed his forehead and smiled. 'Real friends have a way of making their way back to each other. Trust me, true friends will always find a path through.'

Marcus smiled and he gave his mum a **big** hug. He hoped she was right.

Chapter Seven

The rest of the weekend went by in a **flash.** On Monday morning, Marcus, Lise and Stacey sat together in Breakfast Club, waiting for Asim to arrive. All around them, kids were chatting excitedly about their weekends, and the smell of hot, buttered toast filled the air. Marcus and Lise **CRUNCHED** down on their toast, while Stacey scooped up spoonfuls from a bowl of cereal.

Stacey clearly wasn't happy with something. She was focused on her director's clipboard, and after every mouthful of cereal she let out a frustrated **GROAN.**

'How was your rehearsal with Adeya on Saturday?' Marcus asked casually.

Stacey rolled her eyes. 'Not great. Adeya's the star of the show, but I can't get her to focus at all.'

'What do you think is wrong?' asked Lise.

'I have no clue,' Stacey shrugged. 'Adeya's audition was fantastic, but now I'm worried we made a mistake picking her for such an important role.'

'And there's still the problem of the GHOST,' Marcus said slowly. 'If we don't solve the case, there might be no performances at all.'

'Marcus has a point,' Lise agreed. 'Some

Drama Club members are scared it might come back and are thinking of dropping out.'

'Yeah, I've heard,' Stacey sighed, 'and honestly, I'm worried about it too. I want to solve the case, but I also need to make sure the play is a hit. It's a lot of pressure all at once.' She set her clipboard on the table and wearily rubbed her face.

'That's why we work as a team, right?' Marcus said. 'I mean, look at all the cases the **BCI** have solved already; like when the basketball team thought they were ***cursed***, or stopping the Phantom Thief stealing from clubs. It's not all on you, Stacey. We've got this, **together!**'

Stacey lifted her hands from her eyes and smiled.

'There is one other thing,' Lise said with

her eyes fixed on the table. 'The performance is at the end of the week and we've only sold ten tickets!'

The smile **slipped** from Stacey's face. 'We can't perform to only ten people. Mrs Miller will be so disappointed.'

Marcus looked at his friends' worried faces and thought back to his mum's advice. He might not be in the play, but that didn't mean he couldn't support his friends.

'What if I sell tickets for the show?' Marcus said. 'You're both so busy with rehearsals at lunch and after school, but I could tell everyone how **AMAZING** the show will be.'

'You'd do that for us?' Stacey said, her smile returning. 'Marcus, that would be brilliant!'

'Yeah, I'll be the best ticket seller the

school has ever seen.' Marcus grinned.

Just then, Asim ran into Breakfast Club and nearly CRASHED into their table.

Lise beamed up at him. 'Marcus is going to help sell tickets for the play. We're going to be a **SELL-OUT SUCCESS!'**

Marcus turned to look at Asim and noticed the panic on his face.

'Someone has **SABOTAGED** the set!' Asim cried, and without another word, he spun on his heels and sprinted away again. Marcus, Lise and Stacey jumped up to follow him.

'Slow down!' shouted Mr Anderson.

'Sorry! Art emergency!' Marcus yelled back, slowing to a quick walk until he was out of sight.

Marcus and his friends hurried through the corridors, panting hard as they reached the theatre.

'*Oh no,*' they said in unison.

The set was destroyed. Paint was splattered all over Asim's cardboard backdrop, completely ruining his designs, and the floor was a sticky mess.

Asim ran a finger over his artwork, miserably. 'Who would do something like this? It'll take me ages to redo all the backgrounds.'

Marcus went to comfort him, but a clattering sound from behind the stage wing made him stop. The **BCI** all tensed, but relaxed as the school caretaker emerged from the back with a friendly smile.

The caretaker was a strong-looking

woman, with rich brown skin, short hair and a tool belt.

Marcus didn't know her name — she had taken over last term when the old caretaker had retired — but he often saw her fixing stuff or sorting out a mess when he arrived for Breakfast Club.

'Terrible, isn't it?' said the caretaker, frowning as she wheeled a mop and bucket over to them. A big set of keys on her tool belt **jangled** as she walked.

'Did you hear or notice anything odd?' Lise asked.

The caretaker tapped her chin thoughtfully. 'Not a thing,' she said plainly. 'I worked late on Friday, and when I locked up, the set was fine.'

'Could someone have broken in over the weekend?' enquired Marcus.

'I don't see how,' she said, **scrunching** her brow. 'When I arrived this morning, everything was locked up as it should be. Only a **GHOST** could get through those walls.'

At her mention of a ghost, Marcus gulped. He looked around at his fellow Investigators and they all looked as worried as he felt.

'I'm sorry, kids, it seems you'll have to restart the set from scratch,' said the caretaker. 'Will you have enough time?'

Stacey wrapped a supportive arm around Asim's shoulders. 'We'll make time. The show must go on, right, Asim?'

Asim nodded, but Marcus could tell he was still really upset.

'Well, good luck,' said the caretaker. 'I'm going to need something stronger than soap to get rid of this mess.' She tutted to herself as she turned and left the BCI in a dismal silence.

It took a few moments for Marcus to express what they were surely all thinking. 'So, do we think the ghost did this?' he asked.

'Do we think the ghost did what?' a voice

interrupted from behind. Marcus turned to see Lawson and Adeya walking in. They stopped dead in their tracks at the sight of the ruined set.

'This was the ghost!' Adeya announced. 'It had to be. These are the kinds of events my older brother told me about. The theatre is its home . . . we must have disturbed it with our rehearsals and now it wants us to stop.' She hugged herself as if she was cold. 'If we carry on with the play, things will only get worse.'

'We should tell the other actors,' Lawson said. 'Call the whole thing off.'

His words **echoed** off the walls and Marcus glanced at his fellow Investigators, waiting for them to speak, but they all looked at the floor in silence.

'Hold on,' Marcus spoke up. 'The **BCI**

have officially taken on this case. We'll investigate and solve this mystery. The show must go on, right?'

Stacey straightened up and looked gratefully at Marcus. 'Right,' she echoed, before glancing at her clipboard. 'That settles it. We go on as planned and we'll solve this mystery at the same time. Adeya and Lawson, I expect to see you at rehearsals later.'

Lawson looked unsure but nodded.

'But with all this **spooky** ghost stuff, how can you expect any of us to focus?' Adeya protested. 'My mind's all over the place, and I was already having trouble with my lines. I really think we should call it—'

'I promise, come showtime, you'll be fine,' Stacey cut in. 'Practice makes perfect, remember?'

'Plus, we're going to find this ghost and give it a new script to follow,' Lisa vowed. 'We don't run away just because some ghost thinks it can scare us off.'

'All right,' Adeya said doubtfully. 'See you all at rehearsals later.' She offered a faint smile, before she and Lawson left the theatre.

'I think I'll come to rehearsals too,' Marcus decided. 'While you're all preparing for the show, maybe I'll be able to find some **CLUES.**'

'Good plan,' Stacey said. 'Thank you, Marcus. I can't believe I'm saying this, but for the first time ever I really don't want to see a ghost!'

Chapter Eight

Marcus couldn't concentrate during morning lessons. He kept thinking about the ghost and all the distress and destruction it was causing Drama Club. By lunchtime, he was seriously ready to start SEARCHING for clues. He wolfed down his food and hurried to the theatre.

Drama Club was a hive of activity when he arrived. Lise was leading the tech team, testing the lights and audio from the sound desk, and Asim was already making a start on the reconstruction of the set.

Rehearsals were in full swing. Marcus could tell it was getting closer to **SHOWTIME**, because in between scenes he heard the actors intensely going over their lines and cues. Some of them had even brought packed lunches, eating on their knees while they studied their scripts.

As usual, Stacey sat in her director's chair. She urged the actors to project their voices and to make **big,** dramatic movements on stage.

'Hey, Marcus,' said Asim. His fingers and clothes were covered with paint. 'What do you think of the set?'

Marcus nodded encouragingly. 'Looking better already. I'm sure you'll get it done before opening night.'

'I hope so,' Asim said, wiping his sweaty forehead with the back of his hand. 'You've arrived at the perfect time. They are about to rehearse my favourite scene. Adeya's character, the ghost hunter, captures Lawson and pulls back the sheet to reveal his identity. It's **SICK!**'

Marcus raised his eyebrows. He couldn't wait to see Adeya and Lawson in action.

'**POSITIONS!**' Stacey yelled.

Lawson swiftly scaled the stage and dragged the ghost costume on over his head so it covered his entire body. Adeya, on the other hand, ambled slowly up the steps, seeming to WHISPER lines to herself as she approached her mark on the stage.

Stacey leaned forward in her chair eagerly. 'Remember, guys, this is the big revelation. I want to feel completely stunned!'

Lawson nodded enthusiastically, but Adeya didn't respond. She looked petrified.

'Cue the music!' yelled Stacey.

Marcus glanced at Lise, adjusting her headphones behind the sound desk. The music was tense and droned slowly in the background. Stacey roared '**Action!**' and the scene began.

Adeya put on her sternest expression, urging the FRIGHTENED schoolkids back as she crept towards the ghost, who had been tied up on the floor. She tripped over a few words here and there, but from what Marcus could tell, Adeya was doing pretty well. Lawson's ghost sounds had improved too and were actually more scary than funny.

'Time to find out who you are!' declared Adeya, LOOMING over Lawson. Her eyes narrowed as she flexed her fingers and Lawson appeared to be shaking with fear through the white fabric.

But just as Adeya's arm lifted, the background music cut off. An awful, warped s c r e e c h tore through the theatre and everyone in the room covered their ears.

'Cut the music!' Stacey yelled.

'Turn it off!'

'I'm trying!' cried Lise. Her face was
flushed red with panic.

Marcus ran over to the sound desk at
the back of the room, peering over Lise's

shoulder as she pressed every button to try to stop the awful sound. But nothing worked. The **s c r e e c h i n g** was getting louder.

Marcus searched the desk and noticed a thick cable snaking all the way to a plug in the wall. He sprinted to it and tugged the lead from its socket so forcefully he fell backwards with a **THUMP.** The noise stopped abruptly, but Marcus still had an annoying ringing in his ears.

'Do you think it's the ghost again?' one of the actors muttered.

'There's no other explanation,' whispered another.

Still centre stage, Adeya crossed her arms. 'We all know what's causing this!' she said. 'The ghost won't stop tormenting us until we cancel the play!'

Lawson got up and **WHiPPED** the sheet from his head. 'I wasn't sure before, but Adeya's right. This is getting really scary now.'

The actors and crew members looked at each other terrified. The murmurs among the cast grew louder. Marcus could hear people agreeing with Adeya and Lawson.

Stacey **sprang up** and joined Adeya on the stage. She held her hands up. 'I know this all seems bad, but me and my friends in the **Breakfast Club Investigators** are looking into it,' she said, trying to calm the crowd that had gathered at the foot of the stage. 'And when the **BCI** investigate, we never leave a case unsolved.'

'But the play is in four days!' yelled a voice from the crowd.

Stacey breathed deeply. 'Don't worry,

the case will be solved by then. We promise, right, guys?'

Stacey turned to Marcus, Asim and Lise pleadingly.

'That's right!' Marcus said, sounding more confident than he felt. It would be difficult, but he had to believe they could solve this case. He couldn't let a ghost RUIN his friend's play.

The air was silent and uneasy. It was clear that everyone was still on edge.

'I think everyone is a bit shaken up after what happened with the music,' Lise observed. 'Let's leave rehearsals for today.' Stacey looked like she might protest, but a swift look from Asim stopped her.

The student actors and crew members shuffled towards the exit. From their bowed heads and slumped shoulders, Marcus saw they were losing their passion for Drama Club.

The ghost was slowly getting its wish.

Now alone in the theatre, Marcus, Asim, Lise and Stacey huddled together in a circle at the foot of the stage.

A tiny part of Marcus was thrilled to be with his fellow Investigators getting ready to solve a case after so long. He had missed them. He had missed this.

'The ghost is RUINING everything,' said Stacey, staring at her friends in turn. 'It feels like all our actors and crew are this close to quitting.' She pinched her fingers, leaving a tiny gap.

'So that's why we're going to do what we always do,' stated Lise. 'Solve the mystery and catch the bad guy.'

'But where do we start?' Asim wondered. 'The ghost is . . . a ghost that doesn't seem to like our play. We have nothing else to go on.'

'Nothing yet,' Stacey said as the bell rang, signalling the end of lunch. 'Let's come back after school when we've got more time. If we can find out what it wants, we can solve this case once and for all.'

Chapter Nine

Even though the case was his main priority, Marcus hadn't forgotten his promise to sell tickets for the play. So, after asking if he could leave his last class five minutes early, he *RUSHED* to set up a table for tickets at the main reception area, hoping to catch kids on their way home.

The last bell *rang* just as he set out the tickets on the table, and in an instant a wave of students **flooded** through the hallway.

But trying to stop them as they hurried home was almost impossible. Marcus lost count of how many times he was brushed off, and hardly any of the people who *did* stop bought tickets.

He slumped into his chair after another failed sale and glanced at the huge pile of tickets he still had to shift. He sighed. His friends were working so hard on the play that they deserved a big audience. He remembered Mrs Miller explaining that the money from ticket sales would help a local theatre project too. It would be disappointing not to raise as much money as possible.

Looking up, he spotted Oyin and Patrick rushing past. Oyin had a football under her arm, so Marcus thought they were probably heading to an after-school match.

'Hey, guys!' Marcus shouted. They hesitated, signalling that they were in a rush, but Marcus waved them over.

'Hey,' Oyin and Patrick said together. 'What are you doing? Aren't you coming to watch the match?'

Marcus lifted the roll of tickets up to them. 'Not today. I'm in charge of ticket sales for Drama Club's first play. *The Ghost of Rutherford School* is the **spookiest** and most thrilling play Rutherford School has ever seen!'

'Sounds . . . cool,' said Oyin. But Patrick didn't say a word.

'So, should I put you both down for a ticket?' Marcus asked enthusiastically.

Oyin and Patrick glanced at each other.

'What's wrong?' Marcus asked.

Patrick exhaled. 'It does sound great, and I know Lise wrote the script and everything . . . but isn't the theatre HAUNTED?'

'I've heard the rumours too,' Oyin added. 'I'd love to support Drama Club, but if that means seeing a *real ghost*, I'd rather give it a miss.'

Marcus scrambled for the right words. If even his best friends were cautious of buying

a ticket, what chance did he have to sell out the show?

Just as he was losing hope, Marcus spotted Adeya in the passing crowd. If anyone could convince someone to buy a ticket, it would be the show's lead performer.

'Hey, Adeya,' Marcus called out. 'Come and meet my friends!'

Startled, Adeya stopped and smiled. 'Hi,' she said and walked over.

Marcus **beamed**. 'This is Oyin and Patrick. They're interested in coming to the show but are a little on the fence. And so who better to convince them than the ghost hunter herself?'

Oyin's eyes widened. 'You're the lead actor?' she asked.

'That must be pretty cool,' said Patrick.

Adeya shrugged. 'It's OK, I guess,' she mumbled.

'So, what do you think of the play?' asked Oyin. 'Marcus said we should buy tickets, but we're not sure because of all the ghost rumours.'

Marcus glanced at Adeya expectantly, but to his surprise, she only **SHRUGGED** again.

'What can I say,' Adeya replied. 'Lise's script is cool, but being on stage when a real ghost shows up is **TERRIFYING.**'

Marcus felt his mouth drop open in surprise. 'I think what Adeya is trying to say—'

'—is that I am sorry to burst your bubble, guys,' concluded Adeya. 'The play is cursed.' She hung her head and hurried off with her football tucked under her arm.

'Adeya, wait!' Marcus called after her, but she had already slipped into the crowd and disappeared.

Marcus looked at Oyin and Patrick hopefully. 'Maybe we do have a little ghost problem, but the **BCI**—'

'Sorry, Marcus,' Oyin interrupted, with a regretful look. 'I'm gonna have to give the play a miss.'

'Yeah . . . maybe next time,' said Patrick, giving him a small smile.

As his friends walked away, Marcus was disappointed but knew he couldn't give up. Drama Club was depending on him to make sure they had a **big** audience on Friday night, so even if it was tough, he had to keep trying.

★

'Sooo, should I put you down for three tickets?' Marcus asked some final stragglers on their way out of school. Marcus had been talking with them for the last few minutes and knew he was close to making a sale.

'What about the gho—?' one of them began, but Marcus cut in before they could finish.

'I give you my personal **Breakfast Club Investigator** guarantee,' Marcus said, with a waggle of his index finger. 'There will be no unwelcome visits from any ghosts during Friday's play.'

The uncertain students fidgeted indecisively, before saying, 'Go on then,' and reached for their wallets.

Marcus gladly ripped off three tickets. 'It's going to be the best show you've ever seen,' he insisted, as his customers turned away happily. He put their money in the collection tin and glanced at the pile of unsold tickets. It was still quite tall, but little by little, it was dwindling.

'Not bad,' said a voice from the side. Marcus turned to see Mr Anderson, smiling down at him, his blue eyes *twinkling*. 'I see you're an expert salesperson, Marcus! Going well, is it?' he asked.

Marcus exhaled. 'No, it's slower than I had hoped. But I've sold some.'

'I can see that,' Mr Anderson said. He approached the table and reached for his wallet. 'I'd like a ticket, please!'

Marcus had a sneaky suspicion that Mr Anderson was buying a ticket because he felt sorry for him. 'You don't have to do that, sir,' he began, but Mr Anderson frowned.

'Nonsense!' he exclaimed. 'With all the good things I've heard about this play, I can't miss it. Not to mention the hard work I've seen you all put in. I can't wait!'

Marcus nodded. 'It's true. Drama Club have worked really hard on it.'

'Not just them,' Mr Anderson said. 'You too.'

'*Me?*' Marcus scoffed. 'I'm just selling tickets.'

'On the contrary!' Mr Anderson remarked. 'I've seen first-hand how hard you're working to sell these tickets. Promotion is as much a part of the production as anything else.'

'Thanks,' Marcus said, proudly handing Mr Anderson his ticket.

Maybe Mr Anderson was right, he had

worked hard to sell tickets, even when he'd felt like giving up. Just because he wasn't on stage or helping behind the scenes didn't mean he wasn't **important** to the success of the play.

As Mr Anderson left, Marcus glanced up at the time. The **BCI** would be waiting for him in the theatre, and now Marcus was more motivated than ever to catch the ghost. He packed away the remaining tickets and hurried down the corridors.

Chapter Ten

CREAK. CREAK. CREAK.

Marcus's footsteps echoed through the empty corridors. As he neared the theatre's entrance, the air seemed to turn COLDER.

The closed door shuddered as Marcus reached for the handle, and a strange, soft whooshing noise came from behind it, rising and falling like a dreadful song.

OOOoooOOO. . .

The room was dim, but Marcus could see a shadow flitting behind the frosted glass in the centre of the door. *Could it be the ghost?* he wondered, watching the shape dart back and forth. His heart **POUNDED** as he touched the cold handle and the hinges screeched as he cautiously opened the door.

Marcus braced himself for the worst.

'Finally!' a voice exclaimed, almost causing Marcus to **jump** out of his skin.

He sighed in relief when he saw Stacey, Lise and Asim huddled just out of sight by the side of the door. They were waiting for him in the dark, with Asim holding a bright torch that cast an eerie light on their faces. It made them look like they were gathered around a campfire.

Marcus joined their circle. 'Sorry I'm late,' he said. 'I was selling tickets.'

Lise waved away his apology. 'Don't worry, we were just discussing our plan of action.'

'We think that following the noises is our best bet,' said Stacey. 'That clanking came from underneath the stage, so that's where we should begin.'

Marcus rolled his bottom lip between his teeth and nodded. 'Sounds like a good start.'

They bunched together and Asim led the way with his torch. Their shadows LOOMED around them as they climbed up the stage steps.

'It feels like ages since we've searched for clues like this,' said Asim, his voice w**o**b**b**li**ng**.

'I know,' whispered Lise. 'Who knows

what we'll find under the stage. It's like walking into the GHOST'S LAIR.'

'Its lair?' Marcus gulped.

Lise and Asim looked as nervous as he felt, even Stacey seemed scared. Usually, Stacey was excited by the idea of the supernatural, but as they crept onto the stage, her hands trembled.

'Think of the play, guys,' Marcus said. 'Solve the case, save the play.'

The others nodded and Marcus crouched down and tucked his finger into the loop that opened the trapdoor on the stage. It was so heavy it slipped from his grip and swung back, hitting the stage with a loud **BANG** that made them all flinch.

'Sorry,' muttered Marcus.

Beneath the trapdoor were wooden stairs,

chipped and worn at the edges. Marcus shivered. It was like peering into a dark well.

'Who's going down first?' Asim said SHAKILY. The four of them glanced at each other, waiting for the brave volunteer.

Stacey sighed deeply. 'I'm the director, I should go first.' She took the torch from Asim and winced as she lowered her leg through the door. The stairs creaked as she descended.

Marcus went next, trailed by Lise and then

Asim. At the end of the staircase was a rusty red steel door, leading to a musky walkway. Either side of the walkway were large wardrobes that looked like they hadn't been used in years. Cobwebs covered the walls, and long-forgotten costumes and props were scattered around untidily.

'What is this place?' said Marcus.

'It's the trap space,' whispered Stacey. 'Big theatres normally use them for storage, but it can also be part of the play. Though, from the

looks of it, nobody's been here in a while.'

'Except the ghost,' muttered Asim.

Marcus let out a breath. Lise was right before; this was a perfect lair for the ghost, empty and undisturbed. Until they disturbed it, of course. How **angry** would that make the ghost?

A loud crash sounded at the other end of the walkway. The four of them jumped, halting in their tracks and huddling together. A wave of anxiety washed over Marcus. His clothes chafed against his skin and sweat prickled on his forehead as the Investigators *trembled* with fear.

'Look!' exclaimed Lise. 'Up ahead!'

Stacey shone the torch in front of them, highlighting wisps of slow fog creeping forward like ghostly fingers pointing in the dark.

'Has it got colder in here?' Lise whimpered. Marcus felt the chill too. It was as though his body was warning him that this wasn't a safe place to be.

OOOoooOOO. . .

The familiar clanking began again, gradually growing **louder.** In the cramped, dark space below the stage, it was impossible to tell where the sound was coming from.

Suddenly, Marcus noticed a strange shape in the distance. A GHOSTLY figure rose up from the fog at the far end of the corridor, tall, with broad shoulders and long thin arms. It *LOOMED* towards them menacingly. Its posture was hunched and its body seemed to ripple in the air as though it was see-through.

Marcus took a step back.

'What do we do?' Asim cried.

'Don't move! Maybe it hasn't seen us,' Stacey whispered.

All four of them froze, except for the rise and fall of their chests. Marcus's eyes narrowed. Something about the ghost's shape seemed wrong.

'Oh no . . .' Marcus whispered, realizing what it was. His jaw dropped, unable to form the words. Gripped by fear, he pointed a *trembling* finger at the ghost before scrambling back, trying to put some distance between himself and the supernatural figure.

'What is it, Marcus?' Lise said.

'The-the-the ghost . . .' Marcus stammered. 'Where . . . where's its head?'

'Its head . . . it's under its arm!' Stacey cried.

OOOₒₒₒOOO . . .

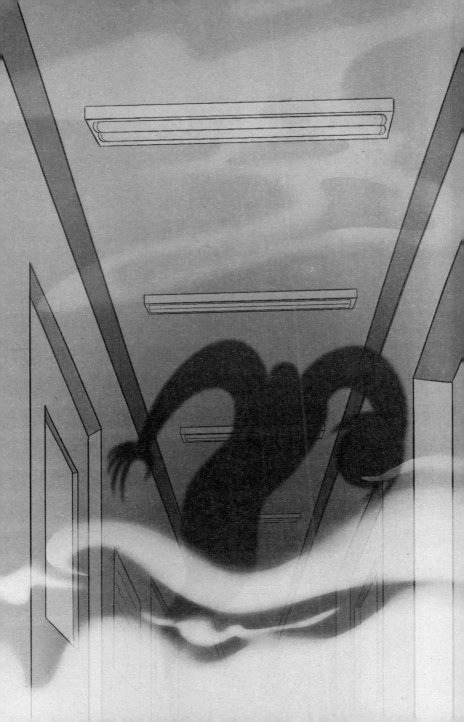

The clanking noise grew louder and a terrifying hollow **HOWL** split the air. Levitating in the fog, the ghost began to lurch forward, closing the gap between it and the BCI.

'RUUUUUN!' yelled Stacey.

The four of them wasted no time and sprinted back down the dusty walkway in panic. Their feet **THUNDERED** against the floor, as they dodged and stumbled over the abandoned props.

Marcus glanced back and saw the ghost hot on their trail, gliding effortlessly through the air. He spotted the light from the trapdoor and willed himself to keep running, even though it felt like his heart might **burst** from the effort.

Asim was the first to climb through the

trapdoor, followed quickly by Lise and Stacey. Marcus sprang up the steps and flung himself onto the stage with a thump.

As soon as Marcus landed, his fellow Investigators SLAMMED the trapdoor shut behind him. Drenched in sweat, the four friends raced out of the theatre.

Chapter Eleven

The next morning at Breakfast Club, Marcus poured a bigger bowl of cereal than usual. He hadn't been able to eat when he got home last night. Visions of the ghost had chased away his appetite. But today was a new day and he needed fuel to continue with the investigation. He carried his breakfast over to the **BCI**'s usual table at the back of the canteen.

Asim and Lise were munching down on their toast, while Stacey was engrossed in her supernatural encyclopaedia.

'It feels like ages since I've seen that book,' said Marcus, looking at the wrinkled and worn pages. Stacey loved to read all about supernatural creatures and events.

Her encyclopaedia had been really helpful in previous cases when they weren't sure how to solve a mystery.

Lise nodded. 'Stacey's been trying to figure out what we saw last night.'

'If I hadn't seen it myself, I wouldn't believe it,' Asim said through a mouthful of toast. 'I was so **SCARED**, I ran all the way home.'

'Me too,' Stacey said. 'Maybe we should have stuck together and written down everything that happened. I think we are a bit out of practice.'

'I didn't write anything down, but I did do this,' Asim said, reaching into his bag and pulling out a piece of paper from his sketchbook.

Leaning forward to get a better look,

Marcus saw a pencil drawing of a ghostly figure, its head held tightly under one arm. 'Wow, Asim,' he exclaimed. 'Your drawing is as good as any photo!'

Asim smiled shyly. 'It always helps me to keep focused on the case if we've got a picture of the creature.'

Lise nodded. 'Me too! Keep it safe and we can pin it up in our hideout with any other clues.'

Marcus scooped up a spoonful of cereal and paused, thinking back to the trap space. Asim's drawing reminded him of how he had felt last night when he saw the ghost. He felt the hairs on his arms stand on end as he pictured the ghost's rippling body and the head tucked under its arm. What type of being would—?

'HERE!' Stacey yelled suddenly, jolting Marcus from his thoughts. She nearly knocked over her glass as she SLAMMED her book onto the centre of the table. 'I've found it. Yep, this is the thing we saw under the stage!' Stacey exclaimed, tapping her finger on the paper.

Marcus, Lise and Asim moved closer to Stacey and looked where she was pointing. Marcus couldn't believe what he was seeing.

It was a see-through figure, with a smoke-like frame and pointy claw-like limbs. Its head was carried under its arm. Apparently, this particular kind of ghost was heavily territorial, and once it claimed a home, NO ONE at all was allowed to enter.

'You're right,' mumbled Asim nervously,

'that's just like my drawing.'

Stacey looked both elated and annoyed. 'A real-life ghost at Rutherford School!' Her eyes lit up. 'If it wasn't threatening to stop our play, I'd be completely over the moon! It's a shame we didn't try to capture it.'

'Capture it?' said Marcus. 'Do you not remember how **terrifying** it was? If we hadn't run away, we'd have been toast!'

'*True . . .*' Stacey mused.

'What's this about toast?' Mr Anderson said as he approached their table. Since the **BCI** had chosen the furthest table from their teachers' prying ears, he often made it a point to swing by to make sure they weren't getting up to mischief.

Stacey quickly closed the book, stuffed it

into her bag and looked up innocently at Mr Anderson.

'I'm getting a **STRANGE** feeling from you this morning,' said Mr Anderson. 'What were you looking at just now?'

Stacey shrugged. 'Nothing important. Just notes for the play.'

'*Oh*, I see. And I guess that is all on a need-to-know basis?' Mr Anderson joked.

'Exactly,' butted in Lise. 'It's **top secret** so the audience will be truly surprised on Friday.'

Mr Anderson's brows lifted. 'Well, if the director is taking it that seriously, there's no doubt it'll be a great show. I'm glad I bought my ticket from you, Marcus!'

Marcus smiled as Mr Anderson ambled away.

After checking that no one else was listening in, Asim said, 'If we've identified the ghost, why can't we tell people? It'd show everyone we're making progress.'

Stacey shook her head. 'We don't want **panic** spreading through the school. Let's keep quiet for now, until we can work out how to capture it.'

'OK,' said Lise, but she sounded unsure. 'We'll keep the discovery to ourselves for now.'

Marcus nodded. 'I agree. I mean, we still don't even really know what the ghost wants.'

'I had an idea about that,' said Lise. 'What if the ghost isn't haunting us, but it's **trapped** and wants our help and disturbing the play is its way of communicating with us?'

'If it wants our help, it's going the wrong way about it,' Stacey said, shaking her head. 'What if someone in Drama Club has taken something from the theatre. The ghost is really **OLD**, right? Think of how much stuff was left around in the trap space. Maybe one of the cast took something they thought didn't belong to anyone, but really it was the ghost's most valuable possession.'

'Hmm. I think it's about the set,' said Asim. 'The fumes from the paint could be bothering it. The paints have a really strong smell, and if the ghost lives in the theatre, it might have muddled its mind.'

'What do you think, Marcus?' asked Stacey.

Marcus scratched his head. 'I keep thinking

about the story Adeya told me. She said the ghost has lived in the theatre for years. Everything was fine when the theatre wasn't being used, but now Drama Club is putting on a play and the ghost wants the theatre all to itself again. Maybe it thinks that if it can stop the play, it'll scare the entire club away for good?'

A brief silence fell over the group as they continued to eat their breakfast. Marcus knew that to catch the ghost they needed to understand its motives, but the Investigators couldn't agree on which theory to believe. His thoughts were interrupted by the clatter of a plate on the table. Marcus looked up to see Maxine, a short girl with glasses, brown skin and braids, smiling at the group.

Maxine was one of the writers for the

school newspaper and part of Journalism Club. Marcus had mixed feelings about Journalism Club. A few months ago, Maxine and Noah, who also wrote stories for the *Rutherford Gazette*, had investigated claims of a GHOUL that had cursed the school basketball team at the same time as the BCI. During the case, the rivalry between the two clubs was fierce, but they got on a lot better now, and had even shared information with each other to help solve mysteries.

'Do you mind if I sit here?' Maxine asked. 'All the other tables are full and I need to talk to you about something.'

'Of course!' Lise said cheerily.

Maxine smiled and took a seat. Asim passed her a glass of water and she set her pencil and notebook on her lap.

'So, what's up? If it's another case, we're kind of busy at the moment,' Marcus said.

Maxine took a large gulp of her water and adjusted her glasses. 'Well . . . I know our clubs haven't always been on the best terms,' she started, 'but since you guys are part of Drama Club, I thought it the right thing to let you know.'

'Let us know what?' asked Asim.

Maxine reached down and pulled out the latest edition of the *Rutherford Gazette* from her bag. 'Noah wrote an article about *The Ghost of Rutherford School*,' she said.

Stacey breathed a sigh of relief. 'Well, that's good, right? Any publicity is good publicity.'

But Maxine's expression gave Marcus a **bad feeling.** She looked almost guilty.

Maxine set the newspaper down on the table. The headline read:

The Haunting of Rutherford School Casts Play in Doubt

Chapter Twelve

'Why would you do this?' Stacey fumed, SNATCHING the newspaper. Her face went bright red as she whipped around to Maxine.

Maxine shot up her hands. 'It's Noah's article!' she said defensively. 'He got wind of the story and published it without checking in with me.'

Lise pinched the bridge of her nose.

'Do you know what this will do to our play, Maxine?'

Before Maxine could answer, Stacey interjected. '*What play?!* We're **DOOMED!**'

'Hold on,' Marcus said, taking the paper from Stacey. 'Maybe we're not *completely* doomed. It's a bad headline, but the rest might not be *that* bad. Let's at least read the article first.'

Stacey calmed down, but the tension around the table lingered as Marcus began to read aloud.

The Legend of the Rutherford Ghost.

Years ago, before Rutherford School was built, there was a theatre on the same grounds. The final play performed there featured an unnamed actor who was cruelly booed off the stage by the audience. Consumed by shame and sadness over their performance, the actor never worked in the theatre again. On their deathbed, the actor vowed to return to haunt the old theatre, promising to target anyone who tried to put on another play where they had so gloriously failed!

According to an anonymous source, the ghost has kept its promise and is appearing during rehearsals. Cast and crew of *The Ghost of Rutherford School* are scared for their safety, with my source saying that if scary events keep happening, the ghost will get its wish and the play will be cancelled! I don't know about you, reader, but this is one show I'm going to miss.

Marcus paused. 'It sounds like this actor could be the ghost.'

'Are there any clues on how we can capture it?' Lise asked.

Marcus continued reading. 'It says that looking back through the years, there are various stories about a ghost haunting the school. It's not just our play, the ghost doesn't want *anyone* to perform.'

Marcus felt a CHILL creep up his spine. The rest of the table was silent, still digesting all the information in the article.

But something caught Marcus's attention. 'Maxine, why does it say the source is anonymous?' he asked. 'Shouldn't Noah have named whoever it was that gave him the information?'

'Yeah!' agreed Asim. 'Noah could have spoken to someone who has nothing to do with the play and who's trying to make trouble, or just made it up! He didn't talk to the writer or director, which is a bit **suspicious.**'

'You're right,' Maxine sighed. 'Noah knows we're supposed to name our sources, and that's why I think he didn't check in with me beforehand. The *Rutherford Gazette* is meant to be trustworthy, we can't just publish anything without having it checked first. It could cause all sorts of problems'

'But you did,' declared Stacey.

Maxine hung her head. 'I'm really sorry.'

Stacey shot up from her seat. 'Save your apology. We need to find Noah, so he can explain himself!' She stormed out of Breakfast Club and the rest of the **BCI** followed her through the corridors, looking for Noah. They found him by the water fountains, filling up his bottle.

'**YOU!**' Stacey cried. Noah jolted upright and gave Stacey a puzzled look as the **BCI** faced him.

'Can I help you?' Noah asked in a surly voice.

Noah was tall, with broad shoulders and short hair. The last time Marcus had spoken to him was when he'd unmasked him as a GHOUL! Noah had been trying to cause trouble so he could write

interesting articles for the school newspaper. It wouldn't surprise Marcus if he was trying something sneaky again.

'Who gave you the quotes for that article?' Stacey pressed.

'Is that what's got you all shook up?' said Noah. 'Now more people know about your play. I thought you'd be happy.'

'All anyone knows is that our play is *haunted!*' Stacey responded.

Lise stepped forward in an attempt to calm the situation. 'Noah, understand that someone — or *something* — is trying their hardest to make sure this show doesn't happen. You played right into their hands by publishing this article.'

'Isn't it the job of a journalist to make sure every side is heard?' Noah said. 'I'd be happy to give you guys an interview too. A chance to tell your side of the stor—'

'No comment!' Stacey interrupted. 'Just tell us who your source is.'

'I'm sorry,' Noah said, crossing his arms defiantly. 'The first rule of journalism is to never reveal your sources.'

'Not even if your sources cause **panic** around the school?' Marcus replied. 'Plus, how do we know it's not you that's impersonating the ghost, just like before.'

Noah's eyes narrowed 'Because it isn't. What, you think I made it up?'

'It wouldn't be the first time,' Asim said.

'I learned my lesson after everything that happened with the basketball team!' Noah exclaimed. 'Look, I swear I didn't make up the quote.'

'If you want us to believe you, tell us who you spoke to,' Stacey said.

'I couldn't,' Noah stressed, 'even if I wanted to.'

'Why not?' asked Marcus.

Noah sighed. 'A few days ago, I received a note offering information. It told me to wait in a dark alleyway by the tennis courts after school. Someone started telling me about the ghost appearing at the theatre and it was so shadowy that I couldn't see them clearly. The only thing I know is that they were tall.' He shrugged.

'What did they sound like?' Stacey grilled.

Noah shivered at the memory. 'They had an **EERIE, ECHOEY** voice. Almost not a human voice at all.'

Not a human voice? Marcus thought.

'Could it have been the ghost itself that you were interviewing?' he said.

Noah didn't seem convinced. 'I don't think so . . . But at this point I don't know what to think.'

'Well, I do,' Lise said, turning to the group. 'It's the ghost. It hates us using the theatre and will do anything to stop us. I'm sorry, guys, but I think we have to cancel the show.'

Chapter Thirteen

*I*t was tall with an echoey voice. Who else could Noah have met but the ghost?

Marcus wasn't hungry, so he went straight to the theatre after the bell for lunch. On his way down the halls, he was stopped by Ana and Clyde, who he'd sold tickets to on Monday.

'Is everything OK?' Marcus asked.

Ana winced and, after a nudge from

Clyde, reached into her bag and pulled out two tickets to the play.

'We want to return these and get a refund,' said Ana.

'We read about the ghost in the *Rutherford Gazette*,' added Clyde. 'Watching a play about a ghost is SCARY enough, but I don't want to see a real one!'

Marcus's brows furrowed. 'But did you know the BCI are—'

Ana cut Marcus's protest short. 'We know,' she said. 'But we'd rather not take the risk.'

'OK . . .' Marcus said, his shoulders slumped. 'The money is kept in the school office and I need to be at rehearsals now, but I'll come and find you later.'

Ana and Clyde looked sceptical, but before

they could say anything else, Marcus was hurrying down the corridor.

'I promise I won't forget!' Marcus shouted over his shoulder. Of course, he would give Ana and Clyde their money back if they wanted it, but they might change their mind once the **BCI** solved the case!

As Marcus turned the corner, he noticed the sound spilling out from Drama Club was quieter than usual. He peered through the window in the door, and instead of people buzzing around doing odd jobs and practising lines, the energy in the theatre was **flat**. Stacey sat crossed-legged in her director's chair, and instantly Marcus could tell something was off. It was the first time he had seen her sitting without her beret and clipboard.

'Let's try this again,' Stacey said, her voice

tired. Marcus looked towards the stage to see Adeya posing awkwardly on her spot.

'Was that last one OK?' Adeya asked.

Stacey rubbed her forehead. 'It was . . . *better*,' she said. 'You just need to speak up. Imagine the audience in the far rows, they won't be able to hear a thing!' Stacey got down from her chair and strode to the back of the hall. 'If I can't hear you from here, you're not loud enough. Try again, and this time speak with **confidence!**'

Adeya fiddled with her fingers and nodded. 'I can feel the ghost's presence . . . It's somewhere—'

'LOUDER!' Stacey shouted.

Looking embarrassed, Adeya started again. 'I can feel the ghost's presence . . . It's—'

'I still can't hear you!' Stacey said, stomping

back to her chair.

Lawson stepped up onto the stage with an annoyed look on his face. 'Adeya's trying her best!' Lawson barked. 'Why don't we let her take a break?'

Stacey put her face in her hands. 'How about we all take a break,' she said. 'But I want everyone back in their positions in exactly ten minutes. Understood?'

The actors murmured in agreement, but Marcus wondered if they would come back. Morale was low.

Lise and Asim approached him before he could walk over to Stacey, who still had her face in her hands.

'It's been like this all rehearsal,' Asim said with a frown. 'We think the pressure is really getting to her.'

'It's getting to all of us,' Lise added. 'It feels like the whole cast is on edge.'

Before Marcus could reply, Stacey appeared next to him, shaking her head in frustration. 'No one warns you how hard directing is before you start.'

'You're doing the best you can,' said Lise, patting her shoulder.

Stacey shrugged. 'I need some **good news.** Marcus, how are you getting on with the ticket sales?'

Marcus's eyes **widened**. He stared at Stacey's hopeful face and thought about lying, but he knew he had to tell her the truth. Stacey would find out eventually, so it was better to be upfront about it.

'I've had two requests for refunds,' Marcus confessed. 'It's the article, it's scaring people.'

Stacey sighed and stared at the ceiling. 'I don't think Drama Club will survive this,' she said. 'It's literally too much drama.'

'What if we moved the show back a few weeks?' Lawson said, joining the huddle. 'I've seen how hard Marcus has been trying to sell tickets,' he continued. 'It's not his fault sales are slow. It's the ghost's fault.'

'But what would postponing the play do?' asked Asim.

'It would give everyone more time to prepare,' replied Lawson. 'The BCI will have tracked down the ghost and people won't be scared any more so they'll buy tickets, and you could fix your set properly, Asim. It would give the actors more time to learn their lines too.' As he said this, Marcus thought he saw Lawson glance towards Adeya, who was now standing at his side.

'That's not a terrible idea,' said Lise. 'What do you think, Stace?'

But Stacey was biting her thumbnail and didn't really seem to be listening.

'Also, I was thinking . . .' Adeya said, turning to a distracted Stacey, 'maybe we could have a quick talk about my performance . . . I'm a bit worried about—'

'**THAT'S TEN MINUTES!**' Stacey yelled, staring at her watch and cutting Adeya short.

Adeya sighed as Stacey **STORMED** onto the stage and clapped her hands. Everyone turned at the sound and all eyes fixed on the director.

'If we want Drama Club to continue and raise money for the Youth Theatre, we can't let these setbacks stop us! Every member, cast or crew must carry on, no matter what.'

'But what about the ghost?' someone shouted from the crowd.

'Forget about the ghost!' Stacey shouted back. 'The **BCI** will handle it.'

The theatre erupted into murmurs until a loud throat-clearing brought everyone to silence. Marcus hadn't noticed Mrs Miller standing at the side of the stage, arms crossed, with a stern expression.

Marcus gulped.

'I want whoever's in charge in my office,' Mrs Miller said firmly. 'Now.'

Chapter Fourteen

'Would you care to explain this?' Mrs Miller said, reaching into her desk draw. The sound of paper crinkled as she laid the front page of the *Rutherford Gazette* down on the table. The headline was just as brutal as Marcus remembered. He felt himself shrinking beneath the headteacher's steely gaze and the rest of the BCI looked equally uncomfortable.

'Did you ask Noah?' Stacey mumbled under her breath. 'He's the one publishing rumours.'

Mrs Miller's gaze hardened even more. 'For your information, Miss To, I've spoken with Noah already, and firmly warned him about the dangers of publishing unchecked statements as facts. But right now, I am not speaking with Noah. I'm speaking with the four of you.'

Stacey sank into her chair as the room fell into a deafening silence. Then, like a dam bursting, the **BCI** erupted into a loud protest, with everyone speaking at once and arguing different points.

'Quiet!' demanded Mrs Miller, bringing her office to silence once more. 'How am I supposed to understand anything if you are all speaking at once?' She peered at each of them in turn. 'Now, what is all this about a haunting? I hope this is not some kind of stunt to sell more tickets.'

'It's not that at all,' Stacey protested. 'The ghost is real, and besides, it's hurting the play, not helping it.'

'It messed up the sound system,' Lise said.

'And it **destroyed** my set,' Asim added.

'It's a whole lot of trouble,' finished Marcus.

'So I've heard,' Mrs Miller said, eyebrows raised. 'I've got it on good information that some members of the cast are too scared to perform, and at the same time, students are too scared to go and watch the play.'

'What is everyone's problem? We have it under control!' Stacey replied irritably.

Mrs Miller frowned and she raised her hand for Stacey's silence.

'Mind your tone, Miss To,' their headteacher said sternly. 'You may be director of the play, but that does not mean you are free to direct everyone.'

As Stacey gulped, Mrs Miller leaned back in her chair and stared at the children thoughtfully.

'How are the ticket sales for the show coming along?' Mrs Miller asked then, diverting the conversation.

As Marcus's friends turned to him, he hung his head. 'Sales are . . . slow,' he murmured.

'That's a shame,' Mrs Miller said, sounding genuinely disappointed. 'The school has been wanting to put on a show for some time, and when I saw how passionate everyone in Drama Club was about putting one on, it seemed like a fantastic idea to give you that creative freedom.'

Asim leaned forward. 'It is a fantas—'

'But!' Mrs Miller continued. 'I must consider the rest of the school too. I do not want reports of pupils being *frightened* by this "ghost", or students gossiping about hauntings instead of paying attention during their classes.'

'We can't control that,' cried Lise.

'Nevertheless, the play is the source of this disturbance,' Mrs Miller replied. 'And I cannot allow for anything to disrupt your fellow students' education. I'm sorry, but I very well may have to shut the play down.'

'**NOOO!**' Stacey cried, her voice cracking.

Lise's eyes welled with tears, and Asim

stared fixedly at the ground. Marcus's heart ached. Though they had considered the possibility of the play being cancelled, Mrs Miller's suggestion made it feel final, like the last nail in the coffin.

'What can we do to change your mind?' Marcus asked.

Mrs Miller raised an eyebrow. 'You know, I thought this might take some pressure off your shoulders,' she said. 'This "ghost" isn't your doing, but it means you won't be ready to perform on show night or sell enough tickets. Sometimes the right thing to do is to walk away.'

'We *will* be ready,' Stacey said. '**Please, please, please,** Mrs Miller, don't cancel our show because of this. We've worked so hard on it that not getting to perform would be the **worst** thing ever. This ghost is nothing really, it's probably just us being **dramatic.** If we stop worrying about it, then the rest of the school won't even have anything to gossip over.'

'Hmm.' Mrs Miller tapped her top lip. 'I assume this is how you *all* feel?'

The BCI nodded. In Mrs Miller's serious stare, Marcus could see the fate of Drama Club being decided. He felt utterly *hopeless* and the ticking clock on the wall only made it worse.

Mrs Miller made a steeple with her fingers. 'Right, I have chosen to keep Drama Club open——' she said.

'**Yes!**' Stacey said, punching the air.

Mrs Miller gave her a weary look. 'For now. But I do not want to hear any more concerning stories about hauntings and runaway ghosts. Is that understood?'

The Breakfast Club Investigators looked at each other uncertainly, but Marcus gave the tiniest of shrugs and they all said, 'Yes, Mrs Miller.'

Chapter Fifteen

After leaving Mrs Miller's office, the **BCI** headed for their hideout to regroup. The cabin they used as a base was ancient, and from the outside seemed older than the school building itself. But the Investigators had given the inside a **dazzling** upgrade, with a couch, chairs, a table and carpet. Asim had even painted a BCI mural on one of the walls. Usually it was their chill-out space, but now it was a hive of nervous activity.

Stacey paced the length of the room, her encyclopaedia open in her hands. Asim was frantically sketching at the table, while Marcus and Lise flicked through previous case notes for **inspiration.** No one had said much since they'd left the headteacher's office, but their expressions said it all:

Worry. Fear. Determination.

Even though it would be tough, Marcus could see how much they wanted this play to work out. He remembered the advice his mum had given him a few days ago. 'Trust me, true friends will always find a path through.' That was it, they had to find a way through, together.

'Guys, make a huddle,' Marcus said, reaching out to his friends.

The Investigators formed a circle.

'I know things aren't going perfectly right now, but it's not over,' Marcus said. 'Tickets are my responsibility and I'm going to spend the rest of the day bringing in sales.'

'But it feels like our play is getting less popular by the day,' said Lise, doing her best not to sound too negative. 'The ghost rumours are all people can think about.'

Marcus paused for a moment. 'Then we're going to make them forget. The play is worth watching, right? By the end of the day, everyone at Rutherford will know that.'

'How?' said Asim. Stacey and Lise looked just as **puzzled.**

Marcus smiled. 'I'm glad you asked, Asim. Can you help me with something?'

★

Marcus and Asim sprinted to one of the Art classrooms. When Marcus had told Asim about his grand idea, Asim had rubbed his hands in glee. Art was his **passion** and the fact it was for the play made it doubly exciting.

They burst into a classroom and Asim started rummaging through drawers and cupboards.

He pulled out a large piece of card, using felt-tip pens to decorate it with **vibrant** colours at Marcus's instruction. Asim had the same focused look he had while making the set, sketching and colouring everything with absolute precision. Marcus held the card still as Asim attached a long, wooden stick to the base as a handle.

'What do you think?' Asim said, taking a final look at his masterpiece.

Marcus looked down at the poster and smiled. The card was bright yellow, with glittery stars and streaks rushing in from the corners. 'GET YOUR TICKETS FOR THE BEST SHOW EVER!' made a striking slogan. Marcus would be impossible to miss.

'It's perfect,' Marcus said, eager to test out his plan. 'Tell Stacey and Lise I'll see them in the theatre after school. I've got tickets to sell!'

After giving Asim a quick high five, Marcus **rushed** towards the canteen.

He hovered from table to table, like a bee in a flower garden, and spun words smooth as honey to anyone that would listen.

'I wouldn't want to be the kid that missed the play and then had to listen to everyone talking about it,' Marcus said to a few students who were mid-chew. 'That would be **terrible!**'

'I'll have a ticket, please!' one student said after swallowing their food.

'Me too!' said another.

Marcus's smile broadened with every sale.

Each time he **BUZZED** over to a new table, the amount of money he had taken grew larger and the roll of tickets smaller. Mrs Miller would be thrilled by the funds he was raising for the theatre project!

The canteen was getting quieter as people finished eating, so Marcus made a break for the library. Mr Fondo, the librarian, gave him a stern side-eye as he **squeezed** through the door, and warned him with a wag of the finger to keep quiet.

'This is a once-in-a-schooltime opportunity,' Marcus whispered, hovering over the shoulders of a few annoyed kids trying to

study. 'Work hard, watch the play harder,' he tried, with a cheesy businessman's smile. In the end, they said yes. Whether or not they bought tickets just to get rid of him, Marcus couldn't be sure.

By the end of lunch, Marcus had fewer than half of his tickets left. He could barely concentrate in Maths and kept glancing at the clock, waiting for the final bell. As soon as the teacher let him go, Marcus shot back out into the hallway, ready to sell.

The corridors were **busy** and Marcus took full advantage.

Hopping from group to group and pitching to anyone who lent him their ear. He even **bumped** into Ana and Clyde who had tried to return their tickets. After seeing Marcus sell so many more tickets, they were happy to keep theirs, as long as he promised there would be only one, pretend ghost on Friday!

Full of charm, Marcus was like a human selling machine, and by the time he made his way to the school office to drop off the money, he had less than a quarter of seats still available.

Both ecstatic and tired, he stepped through the theatre doors and slumped into the first seat he found. The rest of the BCI approached with wide eyes.

'Is this what you and Asim were doing when you left the hideout?' Lise asked, gesturing at the sign.

'Looks good, huh?' said Asim proudly.

'I thought you didn't like being in the spotlight, Marcus,' Lise said cheekily. 'You'd be hard to miss from space!'

Marcus chuckled.

Stacey was bouncing on the balls of her feet eagerly. 'So how many did you sell, Marcus?' she asked.

Marcus pulled out the slim roll of tickets. 'I told you people would get on board, they just needed a bit of encouragement.' He smiled.

His fellow Investigators gave him a high five.

'That'll get Mrs Miller off our backs for now,' said Stacey. 'We know how much she wanted to raise funds for the theatre project.

Now all we need is to catch this GHOST.'

'Actually . . . I had a plan for that,' said Asim. The group turned to Asim eagerly. 'The next time the ghost appears, we should chase it to the storage cupboard where I keep my paints.'

Marcus's skin broke out in **GOOSEFLESH** at the thought of the ghost. He was not going to face it again unless their plan was foolproof.

'How do you know there's no way to escape the store cupboard?' asked Marcus.

'Because I've been in and out of that room for weeks and there's definitely only one door, which we'll be standing in front of,' Asim explained patiently. 'When the ghost appears, two of us will lead it to the cupboard and the others will be waiting to shut the door on it.'

Marcus glanced at Stacey and Lise. 'What do you guys think? I—' He broke off as a sinister clanging filled the room.

The group turned, just as the lights overhead began to *FLICKER*. The stage seemed to vibrate, and the clanging grew louder and **louder** around them. At once, the trapdoor sprang open. Smoke trickled up from the steps, and through it a gangly shape loomed up and over the dark and shadowy stage. Its posture was menacing, spread wide, as if it could reach out and snatch them.

'**BEEEE GONNNE!**' the ghost cried.

The BCI gasped and stepped backwards as one.

Marcus's chest felt **tight** with fear, but he forced himself to breathe and focus. He knew that if they ran now they may not get another chance.

'Asim, I think we should go with your plan,' Marcus whispered.

Stacey and Lise glanced sideways to Asim. 'Let's do it,' they both said together.

Asim gulped. 'OK, let's spread out. Me and Stacey will lead the ghost left, towards the cupboard.'

Marcus nodded. 'I'll run to open the door with Lise.'

The four of them nodded and flanked out to either side. The ghost's **WARBLY** *OOOoooOOO* chants made Marcus's legs wobble at every step.

'**NOW!**' yelled Asim.

Asim and Stacey began shouting to attract the ghost's attention. The ghostly figure turned towards them and **HOWLED** in response, seeming to vibrate with rage.

'Let's go!' Lise hissed to Marcus.

Running as fast as they could, Marcus and Lise reached the storage cupboard door. After fumbling with the handle for a few seconds, Marcus flung it open and crouched behind the open door with Lise. Seconds later, he heard hurried footsteps as

Stacey and Asim tore down the corridor. 'Get ready!' Stacey shouted. Knowing the door would be open, Stacey and Asim slowed down and sidestepped the opening, but the ghost wasn't so lucky. It lurched at speed towards the cupboard and **CRASHED** through the door.

'Shut it!' yelled Lise.

Marcus and Stacey leaped forward and slammed the door shut behind the ghost. The ghost wailed as they pressed their bodies against the frame.

'What do we do now?' Asim asked fearfully.

Chapter Sixteen

Only a minute had passed, but it felt like an hour. The wails of the ghost had calmed down, leaving behind an *eerie* silence. 'What's the plan?' asked Marcus, looking around at his friends.

'We should confront it,' Stacey stated firmly. 'Tell it to leave this place for good.'

'Maybe we should try to reason with it?' Lise suggested. 'This is its home. Maybe all its anger just comes from being upset.'

'But what if it turns on us?' worried Asim.

Marcus bit his lip. 'We should go big. Show it we belong here. Then it will leave us alone.'

Outnumbered, Lise nodded. 'All right, let's confront it,' she said, turning round to the cupboard.

'Shh,' Stacey said, her ear pushed to the door.

'What can you hear?' Marcus asked.

'Nothing,' Stacey replied. She pulled away from the door, wearing a **grim** expression. 'It's quiet . . . too quiet,' she continued. 'Ghosts can go through things, right? Think about how it got in to destroy the set the other day. If it can pass through walls, it might have already escaped.'

'Ah,' Asim said. 'Good point.'

Marcus's stomach **dropped**. If Stacey was right, they may have let the ghost escape while they were talking. Even though he was scared, Marcus knew they needed to open the door. It was the only way to be sure the ghost was still inside.

'Ready?' Stacey asked, locking eyes with each of them as she gripped the handle. In one swift motion, she flung the cupboard door open, slamming it against the wall, and rushed inside. Marcus and the others followed quickly after her. His heart pounded through his chest as they crowded into the storage cupboard, scanning from left to right.

The air inside had an odd COOLNESS, like it was home to something unnatural, but the cupboard was empty.

'It's not here,' Asim whispered. 'But that's impossible . . .'

'Look for clues,' Lise said under her breath. 'Maybe the ghost left something behind when it escaped.'

The four of them crept around, moving paint cans and old pieces of set dressing. Pictures of costumes and theatre posters hung on the walls, and a toolbox sat discarded in the corner. From what Marcus could tell, there was no evidence of anything GHOSTLY.

'Uhhh, you know when I said there was only one way out . . .' Marcus turned to see a sheepish-looking Asim poking out from behind a tower of dusty lighting equipment. He pointed towards an old door, set in the wall. 'I think it's usually covered by all this stuff, so I didn't see it. Sorry, guys,' Asim said.

Lise smiled weakly. 'Never mind, let's see where it goes to. We might still be able to catch the ghost.'

Marcus walked over to the door and tried

pulling it open, but it wouldn't budge.

Stacey punched the air. 'I knew it!' she cried. 'The ghost didn't come past us, and the only other door is locked. It must have the ability to pass through walls.'

The other three nodded **grimly** and Marcus realized their task had just become much more difficult. Because how do you catch something that can slip through walls?

Lise kneeled down and picked something up from the floor. It was an odd-looking device, white with a silver head that fanned out and a red switch you could flick at the front.

'What's this doing here?' Lise said, analyzing the object from top to bottom. Then she flicked the red switch and brought the device to her lips. **'BEEEE GONNNE!'**

Lise said into the machine, and suddenly the chilling voice of the ghost echoed out from it. As deep and HAUNTING as ever.

Marcus, Asim and Stacey gasped.

'Just as I thought,' said Lise. 'It's a voice changer! I bought one just like it at a market a few years ago.'

'But what does an old voice changer have to do with anything?' said Asim, confused.

'This is a theatre storage cupboard, so it could've been left over from a play,' Lise suggested.

Marcus looked at the toy in Lise's hand.

'Or the "ghost" dropped it during its escape. If it even is a ghost . . .'

The Investigators searched the rest of the storage cupboard for more clues, but there were no traces of anything **SUPERNATURAL.** Dejected, they plodded back towards the stage. Stacey switched on the lights and the four of them gathered together.

Asim frowned. 'That ghost better not have any more tricks up its sleeve.'

'We almost had it,' Lise said.

'Unfortunately, *almost* isn't good enough,' remarked Stacey. 'What are we going to do?'

'We have three days until the performance,' Marcus said, looking around the theatre. 'We still haven't solved the case and I've already sold almost all of the tickets.'

'Thanks for the overview, Marcus,' Lise said sarcastically.

Marcus exhaled. 'What I mean is, we need a new plan. We're so close I can feel it, we can't give up now.'

Stacey looked at him and smiled. 'Marcus is right, we're the **Breakfast Club Investigators.** If anyone can catch this ghost, it's us!'

Chapter Seventeen

When he arrived at school the next morning, Marcus's head was swimming with thoughts about the case. There were only two days until the big performance and the *BCI* were running out of time to catch the ghost.

The corridors had a strong lemony aroma. As Marcus turned the corner, he saw the school caretaker in the middle of wiping down the windows. The fruity smell was coming from her cleaning products.

The caretaker heard Marcus's footsteps and turned to him with a smile that deepened the laughter lines in her face. 'Good morning, young man,' she said.

'Morning,' Marcus replied. He carried on walking, but stopped as a thought came to him. 'Do you mind if I ask you a question?'

The caretaker looked at him curiously, and dropped her rag on the window ledge. 'Sure, go ahead.'

'How long have you been at Rutherford?' Marcus asked.

'Only a few weeks in this job,' said the caretaker. 'Though, in reality, it feels like I've never left this place! I was a student here too, like you. My whole family has walked these corridors.'

Marcus's eyes widened. 'Really? Did you ever hear the rumours about a GHOST haunting the drama department back then?'

The caretaker rubbed her chin, and then nodded. 'Isn't that strange . . . I was just talking about that wretched ghost! When I was young, the older kids from Year Ten and Eleven teased us about it, and we passed it on to the lower years when we got older. We used to **scare** them silly!' She slapped her knee and let out a cackling laugh.

'Did the school put on a lot of plays back then?' Marcus asked.

'Oh, yes, all the time,' said the caretaker. 'I have to say though, I never really believed any of that ghost stuff. It was all just fun and games. I remember one time, my friends gave me a terrible FRIGHT. They dressed up as the ghost and chased me and my bestie Christine underneath the stage. I couldn't sleep for a week!'

'I hadn't heard anything about a ghost haunting the theatre until last week. Why do you think kids stopped talking about it?' Marcus asked.

She shrugged. 'I guess a ghost that haunts the theatre is less interesting when the school doesn't put on any performances. No plays, no attention for the ghost. Until recently, of course.'

'So, you don't remember any stories about how the ghost could be stopped?' Marcus asked hopefully.

'No, I'm sorry. It'll be such a shame if the play is cancelled. I was really looking forward to seeing it,' said the caretaker. 'Now, if you'll excuse me, I've lost my keys and must find them before locking up tonight!'

Stacey, Lise and Asim were already deep in conversation as Marcus joined them at Breakfast Club. He barely heard what

they were saying as he mulled over his conversation with the caretaker. Stories of the GHOST had been around for years, but

they had only reappeared during rehearsals for their show.

'You look like you're in the zone, Marcus,' Lise said, interrupting his thoughts.

Mouth filled to the brim with cornflakes, Marcus looked up to see his friends watching him curiously.

'What are you thinking about, Marcus?' asked Asim.

Marcus told them what the caretaker had said and his thoughts about why the ghost had never been seen or heard from before the play was announced.

'When you put it like that, it is STRANGE,' said Lise.

'Right?' said Marcus. 'I say we go back to the theatre during lunch today. We already found the voice changer, perhaps there are more **clues** to be found.'

Stacey shook her head. 'Sorry, Marcus, with two days to go we have to rehearse during lunch. But let's meet after school to investigate. It still gives me the **shivers** thinking about how the ghost escaped from the locked cupboard last night.'

Marcus swallowed hard. The **BCI** versus the ghost didn't feel like a fair fight somehow.

Marcus spent the entire day thinking over the facts of the case. When Lise had discovered the voice changer, he'd started to question whether the ghost really was as **SUPERNATURAL** as it seemed. Yet, he couldn't ignore that it had vanished from a locked room.

After final class, Marcus made his way to the theatre to meet the rest of the BCI.

Stacey had suggested all the actors learn their lines at home, ready for the dress rehearsal tomorrow, so the Breakfast Club Investigators had the theatre to themselves.

'What are we looking for this time?' asked Asim.

Lise began to pace. 'I was thinking about that creepy screeching noise during rehearsals the other day,' she said, walking over to the sound desk where she controlled the audio.

'What about it?' said Stacey, following Lise.

'At first, I was so **panicked** that I wasn't sure where the sound had come from. But I'm pretty sure that it was playing through the theatre's speakers. The only way to play sounds through the speakers is with this,' Lise explained, gesturing to the soundboard.

'I set the music and I checked it three times. So where did the horrible noises come from?'

Marcus gave the soundboard a sideways glance. There were so many buttons and settings, it was difficult to imagine how a human worked it, let alone a ghost.

'Can you play the music again, Lise?' Marcus asked.

Lise nodded and switched on the system. She fiddled with a few knobs, sliding them up and down, and when she finished, the *eerie* music began. It was just as sinister as Marcus remembered, but it wasn't the screeching noises they'd heard before.

'Er, it sounds fine now,' said Asim.

'Yeah, it does. I don't understa—' Lise began, but out of nowhere, the eerie music changed into a warped, scratchy sound, like screams from a haunted house. It made them all wince.

'Turn it off!' Stacey yelled.

'I can't take it!' cried Asim.

Marcus turned to the plug in the wall so that he could **yank** out the cable like last time. He moved towards it, but before he could grab a hold of the lead, the noise stopped.

'Sorted it!' Lise announced. She stood by the sound desk, looking pretty pleased with herself. 'I know how the ghost ruined the music. Someone set the sound to play backwards,' Lise revealed. 'There's a rewind setting on the soundboard that someone must've programmed to come on after a few seconds.'

Asim looked at Lise disbelievingly. 'The ghost did that?'

Lise shrugged. 'I don't know who else would tamper with our audio.'

'It was able to mess with the lights too, remember?' Marcus said. 'And don't forget about the voice changer too.'

Asim scoffed. 'For something that's over a hundred years old, it seems to know all about technology.'

'I'm getting pretty tired of this ghost,' said Stacey, sounding annoyed. 'We've got to solve this case tomorrow or else Mrs Miller will definitely cancel the show on Friday. What's our plan?'

There was a brief silence before Marcus said, 'I have an idea. It's risky, but it may just work.'

Chapter Eighteen

'**W**ait!' interrupted Stacey. She peered around the theatre. 'Let's discuss this in our hideout. The ghost could be listening here.'

The four of them rushed out to the back of the school car park and spilled into the wooden shack they used as their **Breakfast Club Investigators** hideout.

They made themselves comfy on the

couch and Marcus began to explain his plan. It was fairly simple. As usual, Drama Club had rehearsals during lunchtime tomorrow, and since it would be the day before the

show, the BCI were banking on the ghost making a last-ditch appearance to disrupt it. But what the ghost wouldn't count on was that the Investigators would be waiting for it.

Stacey was the bait. As the director, she would get on stage and make a *brave* speech, defending Drama Club's right to perform. When the angry ghost appeared, the Investigators would trap it, making sure there was no way out this time. And the show would be saved.

Simple.

'I think that covers it,' said Stacey, as the BCI finalized their plan. 'Let's go home and get some sleep. **Tomorrow is showtime!**'

The next morning went by in a **BLUR.** Marcus had agreed to meet his friends outside the theatre just before rehearsals were about to start. As soon as the bell went for lunch, he **rushed** through the corridors, getting a few warning looks from teachers as he dashed past. Stacey, Lise and Asim were waiting for him at the theatre entrance. 'Everything OK?' Marcus asked, noticing Asim's worried look.

'Are we sure we want to go through with this?' Asim asked. 'I know we've worked out our trap, but it still could be **dangerous.**'

Stacey, Lise and Marcus glanced at each other. A cloud of uncertainty settled over the group.

'It's your call, Stacey,' said Marcus. 'You're the bait for the ghost. Are you sure?'

Stacey tilted her head proudly 'I'm the director, right? If anyone is going to be bait, it should be me. Everyone has worked so hard on the play, we can't let it all be for nothing.'

'And we've raised money for the Youth Theatre project. If the play is cancelled, we'll have to refund all the tickets,' Marcus added. 'We can't let the ghost win.'

'We'll be right there with you, Stacey,' Lise said.

'**BCI** to the end,' finished Asim. 'Let's go.'

Lise reached into her rucksack and handed Stacey the ghost hunter cape from Adeya's costume. 'Remember, once the ghost goes for you, throw this cape over it,' she said. 'It'll give us enough time to surround it.'

'Let's catch a ghost,' Stacey said bravely, although Marcus noticed her hand **tremble** as she took the cape.

Without another word, they marched into the theatre. It wasn't packed, but it was still busy. Adeya, Lawson and the other actors turned to them as the door creaked shut.

Marcus, Asim and Lise spread out to different ends of the hall, while Stacey boldly headed for the stage. Marcus envied Stacey's confident walk because his legs felt like jelly.

'**ATTENTION!**' Stacey yelled, standing proudly at the centre of the stage.

The room went so quiet Marcus thought he could hear his heartbeat.

'As your director, I want to say how proud I am of you all!' Stacey began. 'This play is so fantastic that I'm already planning to have it performed again and again to **bigger** audiences!'

Everyone was focused on Stacey, but

Marcus kept moving his gaze around the room in case there were any **strange** movements.

Stacey continued, 'I know you're all worried about this GHOST, but I'm not going to let a silly little spirit scare me. We must keep going!'

Some members of the cast gave a *whoop* at this and punched the air, but overall the room felt tense.

I hope this works, Marcus thought, signalling to Asim, who was waiting by the fog machine on the other side of the stage.

Stacey, still centre stage, raised her fist. 'Our play is going to be the best Rutherford School has ever seen—' She broke off as a soft **CLANGiNG** sound made her stop.

Marcus's heart pounded as the clanging slowly grew louder and louder, filling the room with a dreadful din. Stacey turned to the source of the noise and froze as she saw what was behind her.

OOOoooOOO...

Right on cue, a *LOOMING*, gangly figure emerged from the stage wings. The ghost howled and **LURCHED** towards Stacey, forcing her to the edge of the stage.

The ghost was just as intimidating as

Marcus remembered. Its long limbs and headless neck sent a **tremor** through Marcus's body.

'**NOW!**' Marcus yelled, springing the Investigators to action.

Asim snapped the switch of the fog machine on. Marcus clambered up onto the hardwood stage just as the fog billowed out. He stepped forward to stand with Stacey against the GHOST, but he couldn't see her through the haze. How was he going to protect his friend if he couldn't find her?

Chapter Nineteen

'Asim, you made the fog too **thick!**' Marcus cried through the mist. He could hear members of the cast screaming and heading for the exit.

'*Sorry!*' Asim yelled in response. 'I pressed the wrong setting!'

Marcus groaned. The intense fog had a wretched smell and the smoke caught in the back of his throat and made him cough.

'Stacey,
where are
you?' Marcus
yelled hoarsely.
'HERE!'
Stacey screamed.
Marcus waved
his hands through
the air and squinted.
For a moment, he
caught the shape of the
ghost *LOOMING* over

Stacey, then he heard a thump, followed by a pained **yelp.**

'Help! I can't see a thing!' Stacey cried.

Marcus heard Stacey scrambling about on the floor frantically. He rushed forward to help her, but her wailing voice was like an echo. It was too hard to work out where it was coming from.

'Asim, switch off the smoke!' Lise called.

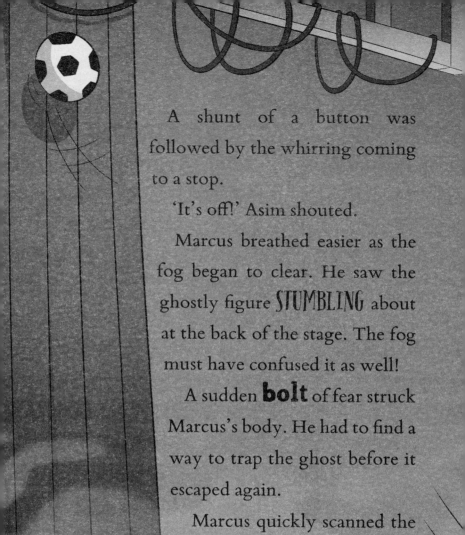

A shunt of a button was followed by the whirring coming to a stop.

'It's off!' Asim shouted.

Marcus breathed easier as the fog began to clear. He saw the ghostly figure STUMBLING about at the back of the stage. The fog must have confused it as well!

A sudden **bolt** of fear struck Marcus's body. He had to find a way to trap the ghost before it escaped again.

Marcus quickly scanned the stage. In between him and Stacey was a football.

Where did that come from?

Marcus wondered, before another thought came to him. Marcus NARROWED his eyes and looked up to the rickety curtain hooks, directly above the ghost.

Perfect.

Marcus darted towards the ball. In one motion, he flicked the football up with the tip of his toes and laced it right at the flimsy metal bar holding up the drapes. The ball hit the bar with a **thud** and sent the heavy curtain flailing down onto the stage.

It flapped and spread out like a net as it reached the floor, covering the ghost.

'**ARGHH!**' the ghost wailed, wriggling and squirming to escape, but the curtain was too **heavy** and held it down.

'Lise, the lights!' Marcus cried.

Lise wasted no time. The bright spotlight switched on and focused on the **lumpy** figure trapped on the stage floor. The final bits of smoke wafted away from the curtain, until everything was completely clear.

'We did it!' yelled Asim.

Marcus smiled weakly. The chase, mixed with a lot of fog-machine smoke, made him feel like he'd played a ninety-minute match. He took a **deep breath** and leaned over with his hands on his knees, watching as the ghost slowly stopped **wriggling**. The **BCI** had caught the headless ghost, but what would they find once the curtain was removed?

Stacey got up and stood at Marcus's side. 'That was good thinking, hitting the bar with the football,' she said.

Marcus shrugged. 'I just did what anyone would have done.'

'If you say so!' Asim said. 'None of us could have made that kick. It was **awesome.**'

'Asim's right,' said Stacey, patting Marcus on the back. 'What would the *BCI* do without you?'

Chapter Twenty

'Is anyone else nervous?' asked Marcus. He felt a cool *shiver* run down his neck to his toes. The **BCI** had wanted more than anything to solve this case, but Marcus felt **jittery** now the answer lay at their feet.

'Yup,' said Lise, climbing up onto the stage. 'For a ghost that can pass through walls, I don't think I'll stop being scared until we find out what's *really* going on.'

A brief quiet took over the group.

'So, who's going to release it?' asked Asim.

'Marcus was the one who captured it,' Stacey said. 'He should do the honours.'

'*Me?*' gasped Marcus. He thought for a moment and then shot a searching look at the lump under the curtain. This ghost had tormented his friends and practically everyone at Drama Club.

Enough was enough.

It was time to end this mystery for good.

Marcus steeled himself and edged forward. His friends trailed slowly behind him, the wooden platform creaking beneath their shoes.

Marcus grazed the rough curtain gingerly with his fingers. He grabbed a handful of the material and **yanked** it up and to the side.

The Investigators gasped.

The ghost had been revealed, but it wasn't a ghost at all! Marcus's eyebrows bunched together at the sight of Adeya nervously TWIRLING one of her braids. Her ghost costume was torn, but from the neck down she was dressed in a flappy white jacket, padded to give it broad shoulders and long arms, just the same as the ghost.

'Adeya . . . ?' Marcus whispered. 'Why?'

Adeya hung her head and let out a sigh. Her mouth moved to make words, but before she could get them out, Stacey marched forward.

'How could you do this, Adeya?' Stacey asked, balling her hands into fists. 'It's been you trying to stop the performance this entire time!'

Adeya swallowed,

and without uttering a word, nodded.

'I can't believe this!' Stacey cried. Her face was pink, and her voice **THUNDEROUS.** 'You're the lead role! Do you know how many other kids wanted to be in your position? Plus, you worked so hard! Your acting was good and you were really coming on with memorizing the lines. Why did you want to ruin the show so badly—?'

'BECAUSE OF YOU, STACEY!' Adeya shouted. Her whole frame shook and she slapped a hand down on the stage.

The BCI flinched at Adeya's eruption and exchanged wide-eyed glances. She sounded really hurt.

Stacey's expression fell. 'But . . . I only ever wanted the best for Drama Club?' she muttered. 'If this performance was a success, it would get the entire school interested. Our shows would get **bigger** and more popular. We could do as many plays as we wanted—'

'Wait a moment, Stacey,' said Marcus. 'Let's give Adeya a chance to explain herself.'

'Fine,' Stacey said, crossing her arms. 'Let's hear it.'

Marcus sat down on the stage by Adeya.

The rest of the **BCI** followed his lead, until they made a semicircle around her.

Adeya gave them all a meek look. 'At the beginning, I was really **excited** to be part of the play . . . *honestly*,' she started. 'Drama Club was my first club, and I'd never been in a play before. I tried out for the auditions not knowing what to expect, and when I got the lead role, I was gobsmacked.'

'But you were so good in your audition!' Stacey exclaimed. 'How could you have——?'

Marcus held up a hand. 'Stacey, it's Adeya's time to talk,' he reminded her gently.

Stacey sat back and pressed her lips together. She gestured with a brief nod for Adeya to continue.

Adeya bit her lip. 'I guess you didn't realize you were doing it, Stacey, but you kept talking about how the show needed to be **perfect**. The future of Drama Club was resting on this performance, so there was no room for mistakes. But it was my first show – I *needed* to make mistakes. The pressure . . . it just got too **iNTENSE.** I couldn't remember my lines or follow my cues. I could barely raise my voice **LOUD** enough so you all could hear me.' Adeya went quiet for a moment, and sniffled.

'It was already too much, and then Stacey decided I needed *even more* rehearsals. At that point, I really wasn't enjoying myself. I *hated* it. It took up all of my time, and even worse, I didn't have time to play football.'

'But why didn't you say anything?' Stacey blurted.

Before Adeya could answer, Lise spoke up. 'To be fair, Adeya did try to speak to you a few times.'

Marcus nodded too. 'Your role as director is important, Stacey,' he said, 'but it hasn't made you the easiest to talk to. Even now you're not fully listening.'

Stacey leaned back with her mouth gaping. She glanced at Adeya, still **slouched** and unhappy, and immediately a guilty expression spread over Stacey's face.

Marcus could see that even if Stacey hadn't meant to, she had really upset Adeya.

Now Adeya wasn't the only one who was **ashamed.**

Chapter Twenty-One

'The first time I tried to say something, Stacey brushed me off and said rehearsals would get better,' Adeya went on. 'But they only got **worse,** and I was already finding them really difficult. No one listened to me, so I didn't see the point in trying to speak up any more.'

Adeya's voice was *shaky* and interrupted by snuffles. Marcus handed her the ghost-hunter cape to wipe her nose.

'Is that when you decided you didn't want to do the show any more?' Marcus asked.

Adeya nodded. 'I wish I could have just quit, but my role was too important. You all took a risk making me the lead, and I didn't want to let everyone down. I knew I couldn't do it, but I didn't want everyone to know my fear was the reason why the show couldn't happen. So I pretended like nothing was wrong and bottled up my true feelings inside.'

'So you came up with the GHOST,' Asim said. 'A ghost who liked ruining other people's hard work.' He had a stony look in his eyes.

Adeya hung her head again, while Lise gave Asim a disappointed glance. 'Adeya seems sorry, Asim, we should—'

Asim quicky cut Lise off. '*Sorry?*' Asim pointed an angry finger at Adeya. 'I worked really hard on that set and you ruined it on purpose!'

'I didn't!' Adeya cried. 'It was an accident, I swear! I was looking for a ghost costume and tripped over one of your paint cans. It **splattered** all over the set before I even realized what had happened. I'm so sorry, Asim.'

Asim crossed his arms in a huff, but Marcus could see that he was taking on Adeya's words. He let out a sigh. 'Oh . . . I guess if it really was an accident, I forgive you. But you really scared everyone, you know.'

'I know,' Adeya confessed. 'But once I started being the GHOST, I didn't know how to stop. I thought if you Investigators saw the ghost, then you'd definitely call off the show. I rummaged through lost property and made a costume out of a big, long jacket with shoulder pads. I held a football under my arm too, to look like a head. I was sure that would do the job.'

Lise snorted. 'That explains the HEADLESS GHOST we saw in the trap space under the stage then. But what about the lights and audio?'

'The lights were easy, and my older brother is a DJ, so he's always teaching me how to use sound equipment.' Adeya frowned. 'When

the **scary** sound effects didn't scare you guys away, I thought making the entire school know about the ghost would work. I gave Noah the quote for the *Rutherford Gazette* and hoped it would frighten kids so they wouldn't buy tickets for the show.'

'If it wasn't for Marcus trying doubly hard to sell all those tickets, that would've worked,' said Stacey. 'Your ghost was pretty convincing.'

Marcus nodded, but what Stacey said about the GHOST sounding convincing gave him a thought. He turned and leaned off the stage to get his rucksack and dug his hand into the bottom. 'I think this is yours,' he said, handing Adeya the voice changer they had found under the stage. 'You must have dropped it when we were chasing you.'

'Oh, *thanks*,' Adeya said, looking embarrassed as she took it back. 'I got this for my birthday last year. It's been pretty useful.'

I bet, Marcus thought. Though with everything Adeya was admitting, something else nagged at him.

'There's one thing I just don't get. How did you get out of the storage cupboard?' Marcus asked.

Adeya reached under her costume and pulled out a **huge** set of keys that looked familiar.

'My mum is the school caretaker,' Adeya said, 'so I know my way around. I borrowed her keys to get into the theatre after hours, and when you trapped me in the storage cupboard, I used the keys to escape and lock the door behind me.'

'Wait! Your mum lent you the keys so you could *SNEAK AROUND* the school?' Asim asked in disbelief.

'No, of course not!' Adeya exclaimed. 'My mum doesn't even know I took her keys. The only thing she *did* do was tell me and my brother stories about the ghost rumours, and how her friends used to play SPOOKY tricks on each other. That's where I got the idea from in the first place.'

Marcus sat back on his heels, at a loss for words. The pieces of the case had come together, but what happened now? The big performance was tomorrow and all they had was a ruined set and a bunch of FRIGHTENED actors.

'I'm in so much trouble, aren't I?' Adeya muttered. She looked like she was trying her best not to let the tears spill down her cheeks. 'My mum was so excited about watching me perform in the play too. I've really let her down.'

Despite all the trouble Adeya had caused, Marcus felt sorry for her. 'I wish you had been honest about how you felt earlier, Adeya,' he said. 'Nobody deserves to feel alone when they're struggling with something. I know Stacey brushed you off, but if you had told someone else, we could have helped you.'

'I can see that now . . .' Adeya nodded. Her bottom lip trembled. 'I really am sorry.'

Stacey cleared her throat and scooted over. 'I'm sorry too,' she began. 'I admit I can be a bit much at times and not always the best listener. But being passionate about this play is no excuse to make others feel like they can't speak up or ask for help.'

Adeya wiped her eyes on her sleeve. 'Don't worry. I know you were trying to help. I guess neither of us went about it in the right way,' Adeya said. 'Maybe acting just isn't for me.'

'That's not exactly true,' Stacey chuckled. 'When I said your audition was great, I really did mean it. I would've never given you the lead role if I didn't think that you would do a good job.'

Lise nodded in agreement. 'Stacey's right. You might not see it, but you're an **amazing** actor, Adeya. You should still perform if you want to.'

'Still perform?' Adeya said disbelievingly. 'You're saying, after all I've done, you *still* want me to be in the show?'

Asim laughed. 'What do you mean? Your role as the ghost is up there with the best drama performances Rutherford has ever seen!'

'Definitely,' agreed Stacey. 'I'm the **BCI's** expert on ghosts and I was completely fooled. You fooled us all!'

'When you put it that way . . .' Adeya grinned. Her eyes locked with Marcus's. 'Do you really think I could do it?'

Marcus gave her a thumbs up. 'I don't doubt you for a second,' he urged.

Adeya smiled, and just like that, a huge weight seemed to **lift** from her shoulders. She stopped slouching and got to her feet. Marcus felt that this was the first time in a while that Adeya had genuinely been enthusiastic about her role in Drama Club. It was amazing what a difference being encouraged could make, rather than feeling pressured to do something.

'You've talked me into it. I'm going to

perform,' Adeya said gleefully and she held out a hand to pull the members of the BCI to their feet.

Stacey gave Adeya a hug.

Lise clapped her hands happily. 'So, team, what should we do now—?' she started, but stopped abruptly at a strange RUMBLING noise gurgling around them.

The Investigators broke their huddle and looked tensely around the theatre. *It couldn't be, could it?*

Slowly, they all turned to Adeya.

Adeya's hands shot up defensively. 'That wasn't me!' she urged. 'I've had enough of ghosts.'

Stacey's eyes widened. 'Does that mean . . .' She spun on her heels in an excitable panic. 'Is there actually a GHOST for real?'

Lise and Marcus gave each other a worried stare.

'Actually . . .' Asim said shyly. 'I think that was just my stomach. I haven't had lunch, you know.'

All of them burst out laughing, grateful not to have another nightmare-inducing case on their hands. The hunt to find Asim some food would be a lot easier to solve than another ghost on the loose.

'Now you mention it, I haven't eaten either,' said Lise.

'Yeah, I'm starved,' agreed Stacey.

With all the talk of food, Marcus felt a sudden **GRUMBLE** in

his belly too. He turned to Adeya and asked, 'Do you want to join us for lunch?'

'Definitely,' Adeya said, looking relieved to be asked. 'Being a ghost is hungry work.'

Chapter Twenty-Two

After Adeya and the **BCI** ate, they spent the rest of lunchtime putting out the word that the case of the headless ghost had officially been solved and that the **haunting** was over. The news swept through the school and a restored excitement about the play spread like wildfire. As the friends made their way through the corridors, Mrs Miller approached the group.

'Is it true? You've caught the ghost?' she asked.

'Yes, well, you see—' Stacey started, nervously glancing at Adeya.

Adeya smiled shyly and stepped forward. 'Thanks, Stacey, but it's OK. It was me, Mrs Miller. I was the ghost.'

The headteacher looked at her sternly. 'Thank you for your honesty, Adeya. I think we need to have a talk in my office. Come with me,' she said, turning to leave.

Adeya followed Mrs Miller down the corridor, giving the **Breakfast Club Investigators** a small wave. The Investigators exhaled as one.

'I know pretending to be the ghost was wrong, but I hope Mrs Miller isn't too hard on Adeya,' Lise said.

'She owned up to her mistake. That's got to count for something, right?' Marcus said as the bell rang for lessons. 'I guess we'll find out after school!' he added, before the group RUSHED off to their classes.

At the end of the day, Marcus joined the cast and crew in the theatre to clean up any leftover mess and prepare for the show. Asim roped in some of the Art Club to help him with the backdrop, and by the time they were packing up for the night, the set looked **brand new.**

As he got ready to leave, Marcus saw Adeya standing by the stage.

'Hey, Adeya!' he said as he jogged over. 'How did it go with Mrs Miller?'

Adeya shrugged slightly. 'It was tough,

but I'm happy I told the truth. Once the play is over, I have to help out with the Youth Theatre project for a month on Fridays after school instead of detention.'

Marcus smiled at her. 'At least she didn't stop you performing in the show!'

'Yeah, honestly, I'm more worried about what my mum will say, but I suppose I'd better go and find out,' she said with a wave. 'See you tomorrow, Marcus!'

Marcus watched Adeya go and looked around the theatre. This time tomorrow it would be showtime. He couldn't wait.

The next day was Friday. All the actors and crew had decided to eat breakfast together in Breakfast Club so they could talk about the show. Mr Anderson had let them pull two tables together and there was an excited **buzz** as everyone ate and chatted.

Even though Marcus wasn't in the play, his friends beckoned him over to join them. 'Without you we wouldn't have an audience!' Stacey said. 'So I think you've earned a place at the table.'

Marcus smiled and looked over at Adeya. She was sitting next to Lawson, laughing at something he'd said. Marcus realized it was the most relaxed he'd seen her since rehearsals began.

As the bell went, everyone got up from the breakfast table with promises to meet back at the theatre for one last lunchtime rehearsal.

The lunchtime rehearsal was a success. There were a few mistakes and forgotten lines, but the cast managed to laugh their way through them. Asim was over the moon now that the set had been mended, and Lise had any technical hitches fully under control.

Marcus couldn't keep the **grin** from his lips. The play was well and truly on.

Before they all returned to their afternoon classes, Stacey marched up the stage steps. Her purple beret and clipboard had made a comeback and she cleared her throat **LOUDLY** to address everyone.

'I just wanted to say how amazing you all have been during these rehearsals,' Stacey declared. 'I for one am so grateful at how much effort you have all put in, and I know how **amazing** our play will turn out tonight because of it. The hard work is done. All we have to worry about now is that we have fun!'

★

'Fifteen minutes to curtains up!' yelled Mr Anderson.

Marcus had decided to check out the crowd queueing in the corridor. Mr Anderson stood in the doorframe of the school lobby checking the audience's tickets. Marcus recognized **excited** faces of students he'd sold tickets to waiting in line. Mrs Miller had even invited some of the teachers and students from Rutherford's ***Journey Youth Theatre*** to come and see the show. Selling tickets for the play had raised over £500 for their programme and that filled Marcus with even more **pride.**

'Hello, young man!' said Mr Anderson, as Marcus approached him. 'You did a fantastic job with the tickets. It's a **sell-out show!'**

Marcus's cheeks felt warm. 'It's easy to sell tickets when a play is this good.'

'As humble as ever,' said Mr Anderson, waving Marcus away. 'You better get going to your seat.'

You're right, Marcus thought, and he zipped through the crowd to his seat. Asim and Lise were just sitting down and Marcus squeezed in right next to them.

'I'm so excited!' said Lise eagerly.

Marcus smiled, but looking out at the

stage, he gasped.

For the first time, Marcus witnessed Asim's handiwork illuminated under the stage lights.

'The set looks fantastic, Asim!' Marcus cheered. 'You did a great job.'

'Thanks,' said Asim. 'I'm just glad everyone was up for helping me get it done. We almost ran out of time.'

'We got there in the end, that's all that matters,' said Lise.

Marcus nodded and then felt the shadow of someone to his side. Patrick and Oyin

shuffled down the aisle, failing to hide their expressions of lingering nerves.

'Marcus, I want you to promise me there will be no real GHOSTS,' Oyin blurted, settling into her seat.

Marcus stifled his smile. 'No real ghosts – I promise. Trust me, by the end of this performance, you're going to be thanking me for selling you tickets.'

Oyin looked at Patrick uncertainly. 'If you say so.'

Marcus laughed and craned his neck around the theatre, which was steadily filling up. Between people taking their seats, he spotted a familiar bright smile.

It was the caretaker, Adeya's mum. Instead of her overalls, she wore a shiny black dress, and was smiling broadly as she read through her programme. Now Marcus knew who she was, he realized how much she looked like Adeya.

Squeezing down the aisle and sitting next to Adeya's mum was a boy in a shirt with headphones around his neck. The boy asked Adeya's mum for the programme, and the two of them riffled through it together with identically **beaming** faces.

That must be Adeya's big brother, the DJ, Marcus realized.

BONG!!!!!

A loud gong sounded. The audience quietened in an instant.

'Ladies and gentlemen, this is your director speaking,' Stacey spoke over the intercom. '*The Ghost of Rutherford School* has officially begun.'

The thick curtains parted and the lights dimmed around them.

Marcus's heart felt like it might burst with **pride.**

'Now THAT deserves a standing ovation!' said Oyin as the curtains closed.

Marcus turned to her with a smug expression. 'I told you you'd enjoy it!'

Oyin said something else, but even though she was sitting right next to him, Marcus couldn't hear a single word. The audience's applause and cheers were deafening. People clambered up to their feet, clapping so forcefully the entire hall began to RUMBLE.

The curtains separated again, revealing the cast holding hands in a row. Adeya was front and centre as they bowed, gracefully soaking up the applause.

'BRAVO! BRAVO! BRAVO!'

Marcus turned to see Adeya's mum clapping happily with tears in her eyes. She looked prouder than ever and even threw a bouquet of white roses that landed right at her daughter's feet.

Adeya **triumphantly** scooped them up and waved the bouquet over her head, but suddenly looked as though she had just remembered to do something.

'Can I invite Stacey, Lise, Asim and Marcus up to the stage?' Adeya exclaimed.

Lise slid out of her seat, embarrassed to have everyone looking at her, until Marcus practically ushered her down the aisle and up the steps with Asim behind them. Stacey emerged from one of the wings and the four

of them stood by Adeya in the middle of the stage.

'The play wouldn't have happened tonight if it wasn't for you guys. Thank you!'

Marcus looked out at the audience, overwhelmed by the sea of smiling faces. The four **Breakfast Club Investigators** held hands and bowed gracefully, before Lise pushed Stacey forward to address the crowd.

Stacey cleared her throat and adjusted her beret. 'This play was a total team effort and couldn't possibly have happened without every single person here. The Drama Club is filled with people with special skills, and without them we would have been hopeless.'

The crowd **CHEERED** and hooted.

'I want to shout out the cast members for

their performances,' Stacey said. 'Thank you, Lise, for writing such a spectacular play, and to our head designer, Asim, who created the best set ever. And last but not least, I want to give a special mention to Marcus . . . Without Marcus, we wouldn't have an audience at all.'

Marcus beamed with pride. His mum did tell him it was good to try new things and with the support of his friends, it felt like there was nothing he couldn't do.

About the Authors

Marcus Rashford MBE

Marcus Rashford MBE is Manchester United's iconic number 10 and an England international footballer.

During the lockdown imposed due to the COVID-19 pandemic, Marcus teamed up with the food distribution charity FareShare to cover the free school meal deficit for vulnerable children across the UK, raising in excess of £20 million. Marcus successfully lobbied the British Government to U-turn policy around the free food voucher programme – a campaign that has been deemed the quickest turnaround of government policy in the history of British politics — so that 1.3 million vulnerable children continued to have access to food supplies while schools were closed during the pandemic.

In response to Marcus's End Child Food Poverty campaign, the British Government committed £400 million to support vulnerable children across the UK, supporting 1.7 million children for the next twelve months.

In October 2020, he was appointed MBE in the Queen's Birthday Honours. Marcus has committed himself to combating child poverty in the UK, and his other books, including *You Are a Champion*, are inspiring guides for children about reaching their full potential.

Isaac Hamilton-McKenzie

Isaac Hamilton-McKenzie is a North-West Londoner who first began writing after graduating from university, and developed a passion for all things storytelling. He has co-written three books for the MG fantasy series, Future Hero, and is the co-writer of *The Breakfast Club Adventures: The Headless Ghost*. When not writing or reading, he loves sports, films, and music.

About the Illustrator

Marta Kissi

Marta Kissi studied BA Illustration & Animation at Kingston University and MA Visual Communication at the Royal College of Art. Her favourite part of being an illustrator is bringing stories to life by designing charming characters and the wonderful worlds they live in. She shares a studio with her husband James.

THERE'S SOMETHING STRANGE
GOING ON AT SCHOOL . . .

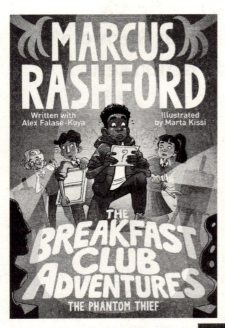

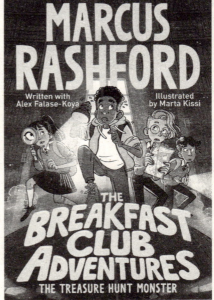

YOU ARE A CHAMPION
Have you read Marcus Rashford's bestselling non-fiction series?

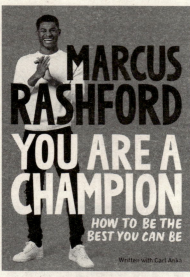

The Number One Bestseller

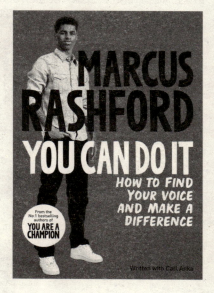

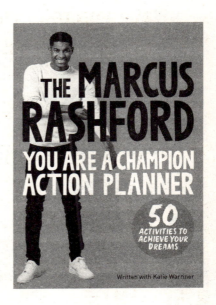

THE **MARCUS RASHFORD**
YOU ARE A CHAMPION ACTION PLANNER
50 ACTIVITIES TO ACHIEVE YOUR DREAMS
Written with Katie Warriner

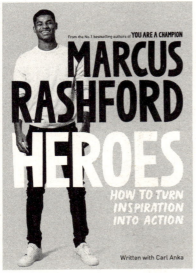

From the No.1 bestselling authors of **YOU ARE A CHAMPION**
MARCUS RASHFORD
HEROES
HOW TO TURN INSPIRATION INTO ACTION
Written with Carl Anka